MIST THE
THE MANOR

Tapestry Tales

Book One

Cara Clayton

SAPERE
BOOKS

Also in the Tapestry Tales series:
Mutiny at the Manor

MISTRESS OF
THE MANOR

Published by Sapere Books.

24 Trafalgar Road, Ilkley, LS29 8HH

saperebooks.com

Copyright © Ros Rendle, 2025

Ros Rendle has asserted her right to be identified as the author
of this work.
All rights reserved.

No part of this publication may be reproduced, stored in any
retrieval system, or transmitted, in any form, or by any means,
electronic, mechanical, photocopying, recording, or otherwise,
without the prior written permission of the publishers.
This book is a work of fiction. Names, characters, businesses,
organisations, places and events, other than those clearly in the
public domain, are either the product of the author's
imagination, or are used fictitiously.
Any resemblances to actual persons, living or dead, events or
locales are purely coincidental.

ISBN: 978-0-85495-717-0

CHAPTER 1

Lincolnshire, September 1342

Clémence Masson gave no thought to what lay ahead. She bounded along the path towards the woods with joyful abandon. Her hair, the same colour as the autumn leaves, was already escaping from her coif. Followed at a more sedate pace by her older sister Agnes and younger brother Mattie, Clémence strode along, carrying her basket, as the bells of the abbey on the Grimsthorpe Castle estate rang for Prime, calling the monks to prayer at the first hour of daylight.

Clémence recognised the trill of a wren somewhere in the undergrowth nearby. She'd learned much about wildlife from Father Robert and took joy from all the learning she'd received from the elderly monk.

Suddenly a voice called out to them. "Where are you off to so early?"

It was young serf Daniel Farmer, watching the siblings from the doorway to his parents' cottage.

"Only to pick berries," Clémence shouted back.

"I was asking Agnes," said Daniel, though he stared right back at Clémence. "You be careful in those woods. Anyone or anything could be in there," he added.

When he frowned, his dark brows met across the top of his broad nose and he looked quite fearsome, Clémence thought.

She glanced at her sister, who moved on with her head down, ignoring the conversation. Although Daniel hoped to marry Agnes, there was no formal arrangement between their parents and his. Agnes cared only for her piety, and as for herself, she wasn't ready for marriage. Surely there must be more awaiting her than simply becoming the wife of a local farmer's son or an apprentice.

"Your work will be awaiting you, Daniel — the day has already begun, you know." The words would sting, and Clémence regretted that, but she disliked the way he was always waiting for them, or watching.

Once again, Clémence was grateful that her father — the master mason and therefore important within the community — had encouraged her to learn to read and write. She could even speak Latin. Perhaps it was because twelve-year-old Mattie had never shown an aptitude for learning, while Agnes had little interest in anything other than her Bible, that her father allowed her such freedom. Clémence adored hearing about countries over the sea from Father Robert at the Abbey, and longed to experience more than this small corner of Lincolnshire. How she would love to visit the great cathedrals of France, see the Frescoes in Italy, taste the spices that were on offer from beyond the Holy Lands.

Villagers foraging for wild garlic, nettles, nuts and berries had trodden the path hard in the sun. A woodpecker hammered with its beak somewhere. Clémence's irritation at Daniel was forgotten as she and Agnes watched Mattie swish a stick at the weeds on either side of the path, no doubt pretending to be riding a steed and fighting monsters.

"We'll have to go deeper into the woods," Clémence said. "Others have already picked these brambles clean."

"It may not be safe, Clémmie." Agnes, always more nervous, glanced around. "There may be wild animals."

"It's well known there are no boar in this area and I doubt a few rabbits or pheasants will harm us." Clémence tried to stifle her impatience. "You'd have to go a lot further afield than even Lincoln to find a dangerous animal. Don't let Daniel scare you."

"He was worried for us just now," Agnes said.

"Daniel takes too much upon himself." Clémence dismissed the ripple of unease which the look in Daniel's eyes had engendered. While it was Agnes with whom he had hinted at marriage, that look was definitely for her. She had noticed similar looks recently on the faces of apprentices who worked the stones or marble for her father, or from sons who farmed the land of the estate. She fought the vanity she experienced when she caught her reflection in the water trough when she filled it for the donkey, or reflected in the butt when she pulled a can for the chickens. On those occasions it was tempting to encourage a few dark chestnut curls from her coif, but Agnes had accused her of immodesty and she had hastily tucked them back under.

"Look at these," Mattie said, interrupting her thoughts. The tell-tale red smudge around his mouth suggested that he had been unable to resist the taste of the plump dark berries.

"Don't eat them all. Place them in here." Clémence held out her basket. "When we have a goodly amount, then you may eat some." She gave her brother a gentle nudge and nodded at the berries higher up. "Pick those, for we can hardly reach and you are growing taller by the day."

The siblings set to plucking the ripe fruit from the branches, taking care not to scratch their hands on the thorns.

"If we find some elderberries we could take those, too, and make some cordial with last year's honey," Agnes said, as she reached into the thicket.

The crack of a dry twig made her start and she scratched her hand as she withdrew it with incautious haste. "Who's there?"

Another snap sounded closer. "Mattie come to me," Agnes called to her brother, who had wandered further away. "Clémmie, did you hear that?"

"It's nothing. Just the movement of the trees. Maybe a dead branch falling."

There was no sign of Mattie and after a moment Agnes continued to pick the berries.

Agnes sees trouble at every turn, but there's nothing to fear here, Clémence thought, as she peered into the woods. Imagination could play all sorts of tricks, and Agnes had enough imagination for them all.

An elder tree with clumps of luscious berries hanging low tempted Clémence further into the woods. She drew in her skirts, clambered over a fallen tree trunk, and picked her way through bracken fronds starting to brown at the edges in the autumnal air. It was cooler in the mornings now, with the turning of the seasons. She reached out and snapped off a rich cluster of glossy purple berries. As she stretched for another, a scream cut through the quiet morning. Clémence scrambled back towards the clearing — and dropped her basket.

Agnes lay on the ground, a man on top of her. Her skirt was pushed up and her legs thrashed wildly as she struggled against him, but to no avail. Another scream brought Mattie galloping but he halted at the edge of the clearing, his hands pulling at his hair, hopping from foot to foot in fear.

Clémence needed a weapon. She looked around wildly. A log green with algae protruded from the bracken at the edge of the clearing. She pulled at it, but it stuck fast in the soil. Then she saw a rock lying under the brambles. She pulled it free and flung it with all the force she could muster at Agnes' assailant. There was a loud thud and a groan as the attacker rolled away, exposing a grubby, whiskery face. Agnes quickly crawled away from him, pulling at her kirtle and apron.

Clémence stood in horror. Had she killed a man? She turned to quieten her distressed brother, who still danced on his feet, crying and scrabbling at his scalp in his agitation. There was another groan from behind her and before she knew it, the man was on his feet. He hauled Clémence backwards, his arm around her waist, pinning her against him, his other hand around her neck.

"You'd try and do for me, would you, missy?" he growled, his breath foul. Fury seemed to engulf him, and the hand around Clémence's throat tightened.

The man's clothes held the stale, noisome odour of the unwashed. Vaguely, Clémence thought that he must have been living rough. Then she began to fight. Clawing at his face and kicking out with all her might, she shouted, "Get off me!"

She found his little finger and began to pull it backwards, knowing he'd be unable to maintain his grip if she pulled hard enough. She heard a guttural, gasping sound and realised it issued from her own throat. She was weakening. Lights flashed behind her eyes as she gasped for air.

With her last breath she shouted again. "Get away from me! Help!"

"What was that? Did you hear that?" the younger of the two men said. "Make haste, Uncle. It was the cry of someone in trouble, I'm certain."

He urged his horse forwards without waiting for the older man. Hooves resonated on the hard earth as the animal crashed through the tangle of undergrowth and pounded the forest floor. He heard his uncle close behind as he entered a clearing and saw a ragged man step away from a crumpled heap on the ground.

Pulling on his reins, the young man dismounted in a practised movement, landing on his feet. "Stand, I say, and don't move," he said, reaching for his whip.

The older man shouted, too. "Hey, you ruffian. Halt and cease your intent."

The young man ran to the heap on the ground and, seeing it was a young maiden, he helped her to her feet. She stared at him, wild-eyed. "Hush, you are safe. This ruffian will not hurt you." He tossed his head in the direction of her aggressor, his flame-coloured hair glowing fiery in the morning sun. "What is your name, mistress?"

"I am Clémence Masson and this is my sister, Agnes." They both turned towards Agnes, who was rising from a deep curtsey. Clémence frowned and turned back to stare at the bearded young man. Her eyes widened.

"Forgive me, your lordship, for you are much changed since we played together as children, but I recognise you now, Sir Ruadhán." She dropped into an unsteady curtsey. "You are returned from your training and the wars with the Scots?"

Ruadhán nodded. "I am, for now."

"Come, Nephew. You can see all is well. Let us be off."

"You will know my uncle, Sir Aedric Amundeville, who has been minding the estate in my absence?" Ruadhán nodded towards the older knight, who was intent on binding the ruffian with rope, pinning his arms to his sides. The man was pleading in a whining tone. "Good sirs, I was but starving and needing food. I have been in battle for months and lost my way. My wife is dead and my child also."

"Silence, miscreant, you will be dealt with, to be sure," Aedric replied in a deep voice as his roan stamped upon the ground nearby.

"Good sirs, I would thank you for rescuing my sister and me," said Clémence. "Please have mercy on the fellow. He has clearly had a rough time lately, judging by the state of him."

Ruadhán saw compassion in the young woman's hazel eyes. He smiled. He was a knight. It was his duty to be chivalrous and gallant.

"He will receive just punishment, but I shall heed your plea and take that into account," Ruadhán said.

"The man's a ruffian and most probably a thief and a liar," growled Aedric, mounting his horse. He removed his foot from the stirrup and kicked the rogue.

The disgraced fellow lurched forward. "Sirs, I was mad from hunger and grief. I meant no serious harm but craved a little solace. That was all, I swear."

"Seal thy mouth, vagrant." Aedric went to kick him again, but the man shuffled sideways, earning a tug on the rope that bound him. "Come, Nephew, I shall decide his fate upon our return."

"I shall see to the matter, Uncle, as it occurred on my estate."

Ruadhán's words earned him a scowl. He may be back from the wars but he had still the battle to regain his authority. Sir Aedric had arrived after his brother, Ruadhán's father, had died. He had been minding the Grimsthorpe Castle estate while Ruadhán had been away in Scotland, fighting for his king. But now he was back, and although Ruadhán had not yet reached his majority, he could manage without the older man.

He strode across to the fallen basket and, swinging it up by the handle, he passed it to Clémence. "I'm sorry you must retrieve what you already picked, but it should be all right, having landed on the dry grass."

"Thank you, sir," she answered. "My sister and brother will help."

"Good day to you," Ruadhán said, and swung himself up onto his horse.

Clémence watched as the two men rode away in the direction of the manor house, the ruffian stumbling along after them, trying to keep pace.

What things he must have seen and what deeds he must have achieved. Oh, how I would welcome such a life, Clémence thought to herself.

Agnes came and stood next to her. "I shall never lie with a man. I know now that my calling is the right one," she whispered. "God saved us, and I shall repay his mercy."

It was Ruadhán who saved us. Clémence smiled at the irreverence of her thought. "Mattie, come." She beckoned to her brother. "We are safe. Help us pick up the fruit or we shall have no cordial and no dessert. We must say nothing to Mother. She will only worry and she needs to conserve her strength. And she may stop us from going into the woods again. You want more cordial, don't you? And fruit pies?"

Mattie's face displayed his disquiet, but he nodded solemnly.

Then, as they walked on in quiet contemplation, Clémence's mind was elsewhere.

CHAPTER 2

Merek Masson enjoyed the freedoms his position as a *sokeman* gave him. He was not subject to the same restrictions on marriage or movement as the serfs, making it easier for him to earn his living with greater ease, as well as the right to buy and sell land.

His last name derived from ancestors employed in the same trade in ancient France as he was now. His forefathers had settled on Grimsthorpe land, which the king had awarded to the de Beaumonts after Gilbert de Gant died. It was de Gant who had built King John's Tower and the small castle on the ridge overlooking the main route north, two centuries before.

The larger castle at Folkingham was three hours' walk away. The first baron had hardly been there, preferring his other lands. While the baron had been favoured by both Edward II and Edward III, he was not the owner but tenant-in-chief for the two kings. As a result, he had chosen not to spend any money made from his vast flocks of Lincolnshire Longwools, and his tythes, on the town or his estates, investing instead in the local church and an alehouse — the first to ensure his spiritual wellbeing, and the second his temporal wellbeing. His son, Sir John, had been lord for only two years before he passed away at a tender age. Now a baby of two had the title of Lord Henri, 3rd Baron de Beaumont, and the Estate was ruled on his behalf by trusted lords since, he, with his mother Eleanor of Lancaster, Countess of Arundel and Warenne was frequently an absentee landlord.

Having travelled extensively while learning his trade, Merek also knew that in this area of Lincolnshire there were more sokemen than elsewhere in England, many having descended from the times of the Danelaw. The freedom and the work suited him well. He contemplated all this as he sat outside his cottage, beating patterns into the lid of a copper box he was making. He greeted another man who was already about his business. "Good day, Roger. Looks set to be fair." He gazed out at the wide skies which stretched into the distance across the flat Fen lands.

"Indeed, and we need it to get the last of the harvest in. Sir Aedric won't be best pleased if it goes to ruin at this late stage. It's late as it is. He may be a knight, but chivalry doesn't fit well on his shoulders." Roger lowered his voice. "I do believe things do not go well between him and his nephew, now recently returned."

Merek nodded in response, but said nothing. Merek's immediate overlord was the knight, Sir Ruadhán Amundeville.

"You've been busy since the abbey moved from over Castle Bytham to Grimsthorpe. What with that and permission from King Edward to crenellate the castle at Folkingham, there's plenty of work for thee."

"Aye, I've been fortunate. Times have been hard for many, what with the old king constantly at war, and this one, too, and Sir John de Beaumont spending so little."

Roger huffed. "Things don't change much for us. Still battles to be fought, especially with the Scots."

"Aye, we all hoped for better, for it could not be much worse with rising taxes and poor weather destroying the crops," Merek added. "The new king is young even now and still fighting, as you say." Although far from the capital, the countrymen knew what went on at court.

"Compared to thee and me, he's young," Roger laughed. "When he came to the throne it was almost the same situation we have here, with our young Sir Ruadhán and his uncle, Aedric."

"Ruadhán may be a knight, and old enough to fight, but he's still two years off his majority, so Sir Aedric will remain here, I suppose. Rumour has it that's he's much more comfortable here than on his own lands." Merek shrugged and stood up. "Ah well, best get on."

"Are you to Folkingham Castle again?"

"No, to King John's Tower here at Grimsthorpe. A small repair to finish, and Abbot Walter at Vallis Dei wants to see me," Merek said.

"I hear they do call the abbey Vaudey these days." Roger crossed himself. "The Latin name Vallis Dei — Valley of God — has all but disappeared now." Then he asked, "Your Catherine all right, this time around, I hope?"

"All good so far. Shouldn't be long now. We're hoping for a boy."

Roger smiled. "God go with you all."

"And with you, my friend." Merek waved at the retreating figure.

At that moment, Clémence bounded from the cottage doorway and kissed her father on his whiskery cheek. "We have the berries to prepare that we got yesterday. It'll give Mother a break. She's so near her time, she needs her rest."

"You're a good girl, Clémmie. Is your sister about yet?"

"Agnes is saying her prayers again."

"I hope you said yours," Merek admonished.

"Of course, I did, but Agnes takes so long. And did you know, she's started wearing a belt of woven goat's hair? It's making her waist quite red."

"She takes her religion seriously, though what she needs to scourge herself for, I know not. She never so much as sets a foot wrong. Takes after her mother. God rest her soul."

"Well, *my* mother needs some rest, so I'll go and tell Agnes to come, and I'll fetch Mattie. Have you broken your fast, Father?"

"Yes, child, thank you. There's bread in the box and goat's milk in the jug, enough for the three of you. You must all stay healthy. We rely on you at the moment."

Clémence and Agnes set about the task of preparing the elderberries.

"You sit, Mother," Clémence said. "Agnes and I shall do this task. You must rest."

Her mother, Catherine, sat down on the bench by the small window and picked up the kerchief on which she was turning a hem. She prided herself on being smart for the Sunday communion. After all, she was married to the Master Mason, and had a position to maintain. Their cottage and parcel of land reflected that. Recently, she had missed church due to her condition, unlike Agnes, who went each day. Her husband and daughter Clémence were not so punctual.

"Ensure you remove all the stalks — they will spoil the cordial with their bitterness. And we don't need illness on top of everything else," said Catherine.

"Why ill?" Mattie turned an anxious face towards his mother.

"They're toxic, my dear. But have no fear," Catherine ruffled his hair, "Agnes and Clémmie know what they are doing."

Mattie smiled at her.

"We haven't made you poorly yet, have we?" Agnes set the bowl on the table.

16

The family continued with their chores, and as the sun reached its zenith, Merek appeared.

"Home so soon, my dear?" asked Catherine.

"I set the men to work at Grimsthorpe. Some stones need replacing on the west façade of King John's Tower. It hardly seems useful to keep the place garrisoned. I understood the need during The Anarchy, but now?"

"What was The Anarchy?" Mattie's voice piped.

"The Anarchy was a dispute between two grandchildren of William the Conqueror: the Empress Matilda and Stephen of Blois, who both believed that they were next in line for the throne following the death of King Henry I's heir, William Adelin, aboard the *White Ship* in 1120. It led to civil war and years of bloody battles.

"Lord de Gant built King John's Tower and castle to protect the north-south routes. Its name came later, for another king." Merek paused. "There's been much disruption and fighting with the Scots recently. Perhaps we do still need the Tower and garrison at Grimsthorpe for safety. After all, it has an advantageous position on that ridge.

"Anyway, as I was saying," Merek continued, "the Tower is a small job. Then I went to see Abbot Walter. He wants a new extension to the wool-house."

"I heard that finances were not so good at the abbey nowadays," said Catherine. "Mind you're not left with a huge bill to pay the workers on their behalf."

"The abbot from the Mother House in Yorkshire visited last month —"

"What, from Fountains Abbey? He came all this way?" Catherine cut in.

Merek shrugged. "It is his duty. He must have approved the building work. They had a surplus of twenty-five sacks of wool last year. They need the space, I suppose, for the extra washing, and drying. The ships queue up at Boston and King's Lynn, all the way from Flanders, you know."

"I know that, and even merchants from the Florentine, but it doesn't mean they aren't losing money."

Clémence had been listening keenly and could not resist asking, "Why are they losing money if they have a surplus of wool?"

"The cost of transport to the ports is expensive. The abbey must pay for the carriages, and the harbour at Boston is constantly silting up."

"We're fortunate that the Yorkshire Mother House still supports Vaudey," Catherine said.

Merek nodded. "Abbot Walter also said he wants me to carve some statuary for the abbey."

Catherine thrust her sewing to one side and clapped her hands. "Oh, how wonderful. Praise be to God." She made the sign of the cross.

"What is the subject to be? Will you use the Barnack limestone or something from the quarry at Grimsthorpe?" Agnes' face shone with rapturous fervour at the news.

"It's to be of black marble from our very own quarry, and the subject will be placed in the refectory."

"Not in the chapel?" Agnes sounded aggrieved.

"My sculptures will be placed around the limestone pulpit of the refectory, in the small arches already carved there. When the monks and lay brothers gather together to eat, they will look up to the reader and see my work. It is a great honour."

"Indeed it is, Husband. And have you the subject?"

"It is to be the seven plants from the promised land plus the fishes and loaves. Wheat and barley will be no problem. Vines, olives, and dates also, but not so pomegranates. I may need to ask permission of Sir Aedric to view his dining table." Merek laughed. "I did see some on my travels through France and Spain as a young man, but that was many moons past, of course." He paused before speaking again. "Speaking of Sir Aedric, I saw him yesterday. He appeared to be dragging some poor soul along behind his horse. A prisoner from somewhere, perhaps."

Mattie began to shuffle, and the two sisters shared a glance.

Merek frowned and looked at Clémence. "Do you know something of this?"

Agnes spoke first. "Father, we did not want to distress mother, but…"

"Yes?"

The events of the previous morning all tumbled out, laid bare before their parents.

"He was a poor ruffian," Clémence said. "The young lord, Ruadhán, who is returned, said he would be merciful, although the fellow would have to be punished."

Beyond her first gasp of shock, Catherine had remained quiet. Now she spoke. "Husband, I think you should go to the manor house to enquire what punishment he has received. I will feel unsafe until we know his lordship has banished this varmint."

"I could come with you, Father," Clémence said. "I should like to see Aunt Joan, to have her recipe for a birthing tisane. When last she and I spoke, it sounded a good thing for Mother."

Merek's sister Joan had originally been launderess at the castle, with several maids working under her. When Ruadhán's father passed away and Aedric took up residence in Ruadhán's absence, however, he had deemed it necessary to have a woman to take on a wider role. As housekeeper, Joan now oversaw the butler, the pantler, the cook and her scullions, the launderess, the spicer, the poulterer, the confectioner and the cellarer. She knew everything that occurred in the castle and its surrounds. She was an extremely useful source of information. At first there had been much speculation about her position, but Aedric appointed a seneschal for the finances and all talk died. Thus, he'd managed to release several members of staff and saved money. All believed he was increasingly satisfied with the comfortable life he was gradually carving for himself at his nephew's expense.

"Very well, Daughter. We shall go together once we have eaten."

Clémence barely managed to hide her excitement. Thoughts of Ruadhán crowded her mind, despite their difference in station. He captivated her imagination. He had travelled and seen the wider world. He had been in battle. He was gallant but handsome, too. And he had rescued her.

"The pottage is ready," Catherine said, interrupting Clémence's daydream. "In fact, it's more of a mortrew than a pottage, as while you were all out yestermorn, Goodwife Margaret brought me some scrag of lamb."

The women cleared the table of the morning's tasks and prepared to eat.

Clémence picked at her food, her stomach tense as she remembered the warmth of Ruadhán's hands as he raised her from the ground to stand before him. The look in his blue eyes carried merriment and … something else. Yes, it was most definitely that same appreciation she had seen in the eyes of the other young men. Her heart began to beat a little faster.

CHAPTER 3

Clémence would have liked to have donned her Sunday dress, but her mother and Agnes would have become suspicious. Instead, she had brushed her skirt and found a kerchief of a more becoming colour than the one she wore for her work around the house.

"I'm ready, Father."

"We must make speed," Merek said. "It's a good walk to the honourial manor of the Amundevilles." He gave it its full title as if he was proud to be part of the demesne. Clémence smiled at the small display of conceit and wondered vaguely if any monk would hear of it through the confessional. She doubted it.

"If we stay until we hear the bell for Vespers, we'll be home before sunset," her father continued. "I haven't seen Joan for many moons. Her role as housekeeper keeps her busy. She will have much knowledge of what has been occurring. The old Lord de Beaumont's father may have had the ear of the previous king again, after his banishment, but all did not go well for him. I suppose things have been more settled with Lord John in residence, but now the baby, Henry, is baron. I should like to know how things fare."

"I wasn't born when Lord Henry was told to leave the kingdom," Clémence said.

"He associated too closely with Piers Gaveston, who was excessive in his extravagance. But it was several years ago and then Lord de Beaumont became one of the 'disinherited' and forfeited all his lands in Scotland after the battle at Bannockburn. He became much more careful, they say, and since then the king has relied greatly on his experience in battle."

"But now the baby, Henry, has lands all over the place, not just here in Lincolnshire. It's a lot for a small child."

"Indeed. Much property and land came with the first baron's wife, Alice Comyn, Countess of Buchan, upon their marriage, and she also brought him the earldom. He inherited his sister's manors, too. Then there were the estates at Sempringham, of course, when the foolish Robert de Birthorpe had to forfeit his lands."

"Why foolish?"

"He should have known that to attack such a holy house as Sempringham Priory would be unacceptable to the king."

Clémence's thoughts turned yet again to the young knight, Ruadhán Amundeville, who was liegeman to the earl's family. No doubt he would have to return to battle before too long — the de Beaumont's were loyal to the king. The loss of land in Scotland must have angered such proud and powerful men. She hoped, however, that it would not be soon.

Father and daughter were hot and thirsty as the fortified manor came into view. They crossed the wooden bridge over the moat and entered the ward through a small door set into a much larger, sturdy oak door. As they stated their business, Clémence gazed around at all the people. The manor house was busy with a variety of activities. A young girl sat milking a goat, while another animal stood tethered nearby, awaiting its turn. Creamy jets spurted from the goat's udder and hit the side of the bucket. Another servant headed across the courtyard with a wooden barrel jug covered by a cloth. Beer rather than butter, Clémence presumed. A horse stood flicking its tail and stamping a hind leg to rid itself of flies. It looked familiar, and Clémence's heart jumped. It was Ruadhán's horse, but there was no sign of the young man with the fiery hair.

They entered the great hall via a studded oak door. A fire blazed at one end, for despite the sunny weather, it was chill within the thick stone walls. At the opposite end of the hall, a staircase led up to what Clémence knew would be the solar. Perhaps Ruadhán would be up there, in the privacy of the family's living and sleeping quarters. The sounds of pans clattering from behind a screened area next to the fireplace told them the way to the kitchens. The smell of roasting meat tempted Clémence's nostrils and made her mouth water as they entered the busy kitchen. A boy sitting near the fire turned a handle that moved a chain that rotated a wheel high up. The mechanism rotated the meat above the flames. The lad was red in the face and Clémence imagined he must be hot and thirsty. The louvre in the ceiling allowed smoke and steam to escape, but it didn't seem very effective at that moment.

A young maid stopped what she was doing and approached them.

"We're looking for Goodwife Smith," Merek said.

"Who shall I say wants her?" the girl asked. She looked to be no more than nine or ten years of age.

"What you up to? Get back to your task," an older woman chided.

The girl stretched up to speak into her superior's ear. "They want Joan."

It wasn't long before Merek's sister arrived. She waddled towards them on swollen ankles, not helped by her generous girth. She nodded at Merek. "Brother. What brings you here?"

"We came for news of the miscreant. I don't doubt you have heard about what happened yesterday."

"Oh yes." Joan looked at Clémence. "Your sister all but lost her maidenhood."

"It didn't come to that, Aunt," Clémence said, "and we were unhurt. Sir Ruadhán said he would show clemency. The fellow had clearly been sleeping rough for some time and had lost his wife and child."

Joan sniffed. "That's not all he's lost now."

Clémence frowned in puzzlement.

"Hauled up over a beam in the barn, I heard. He's gone unshriven to Hell. He's hanging there still if you want to go and take a look — before they take him down and bury him outside the castle wall."

Clémence gasped and clutched her father's arm. "But Sir Ruadhán said he would show leniency." She was suddenly angry. "That's so unfair. It's not right."

"Keep your voice down." Joan spoke firmly. "It was Sir Aedric's decision and he had it done with all speed. The fellow was an outlaw and Sir Aedric was well within his rights. I don't think the young lord knew anything about it until all was done. The lad is a stripling. He has not yet reached his majority, and his uncle makes the decisions around here. It was lucky that their lordships were passing your way. Be grateful that they were, with rogues and outlaws so close to home."

"Surely now that Sir Ruadhán is returned, Sir Aedric will return to his own property —" Clémence began.

"Hush child," said Merek. "Say no more. The deed is done. You cannot question the judiciary of a lord on his own manor lands."

Except these are not his lands, Clémence thought.

"Some ale, Brother?" Joan asked.

"Thank you. We are hot and thirsty after our walk."

They found space on a bench and Joan fetched the refreshment. Clémence sat quietly while her father and aunt conversed. She couldn't forget the image of the poor rogue that Joan's words had conjured.

Her ears pricked when Joan mentioned her rescuer's name. "Arguing all over the house they were. Could hear them shouting. The young one challenging the old, I reckon."

Merek lowered his voice. "Perhaps Aedric's past resentment — about not inheriting, I mean — is catching up with the present?"

"He is wholly deserving, Brother," Joan said with vehemence. "Sir Ruadhán swoops in and Sir Aedric is supposed to simply give all way?"

"It's the law of primogeniture, Sister."

"Pfft!"

Conversation moved on to the fighting in Scotland and troubles in France, and all too soon the time for Vespers approached. Merek and Clémence made to leave.

The short corridor back to the great hall was dark and when they entered the cavernous space the brightness was dazzling, making Clémence squint. Sir Aedric was lounging in a chair near the fire, a wine cup in his hand. "Well, well. Who do we have here?"

Lord Ruadhán stood against the mantelpiece. He looked up from a piece of wood he was whittling.

"It's the little miss we rescued yesterday, Nephew. Come and stand before me, girl," Aedric said.

Clémence glanced at her father, who gave a small nod.

"How is your sister? From a different mould to you, I see." Aedric's gaze swept over her. She met his eyes with her own steadfast gaze and he laughed.

"Sirs," Merek said, "we must away. It's a goodly walk and if we are to be home before sunset we must leave now. We did but come to seek my sister Joan, your housekeeper, and to discern the fate of the man who attacked my daughters yesterday."

Clémence could not resist speaking. "You said the man would receive just punishment, but we have learned that was not to be."

"He got what he deserved," barked Sir Aedric. "I might argue it could have gone much worse for him, but in the end it was quick enough."

Sir Ruadhán turned to Merek. "I will see you on your way."

As he strode away, Clémence could not help but admire the way that his russet-coloured hair, longer than the fashion of the day, fell in tousled curls onto broad shoulders. He turned as they neared the large oak door through which they had entered, and their eyes met briefly.

Her father was already passing through the door. As she turned to follow, Ruadhán thrust out his hand. "Here," he said, passing her a small wooden carving.

Clémence looked up at him in surprise, but Ruadhán had already turned away. She quickly secreted the object into the small bag at her waist, to study later.

Clémence said little on the long walk home. Sir Aedric had riled her with his arrogant stare, and his words showed no pity or understanding for humanity.

After a while she asked her father what he had meant when he'd asked Joan if Sir Aedric's past resentment was catching up with the present.

"He always thought he and his brother — Sir Ruadhán's father — would have an equal share when their father passed, because they were twins," replied Merek. "But the law is clear. The eldest son inherits all, even if it is only by a matter of minutes."

"So Sir Ruadhán is the rightful heir to the manor house and all its lands?"

"Yes, from his father, the elder twin."

"No wonder Sir Aedric is cross about it."

On nearing their home, they chanced to meet Daniel. His clothes were sweat-stained and dirty after a day of manual labour, and Clémence couldn't help comparing his stocky build, square palms and dirty hands, with Ruadhán's tall, slim figure and clean nails. He stared at them, his brows drawn together in a perpetual frown.

"How was your work today, Daniel?" Merek asked. "I gather you were clearing the new patch of land your father has acquired."

"It's done," Daniel said shortly. Then he asked, "Have you heard the fate of the rogue from yesterday?"

Merek told him what they learned. "We are come from the manor now."

"Drawing and quartering would have been too good for him," the younger man muttered, looking at Clémence.

"It's over and too late for aught else," snapped Clémence. "Sir Ruadhán understood the wretch had suffered and was sorry, but not so his uncle. I want to hear no more of it." She ignored the scowl on Daniel's face and turned towards home.

Upon her arrival she saw they had a visitor and she dropped a curtsey to the old man. "Father Robert, I am pleased to see you." The monk placed a hand upon her head as she knelt before him in reverence. It rested heavily, a testament to his age, but she minded not. Father Robert had been a part of her life since the day she was born. Her mother had been ill following her birth, and the good monk had visited every day, and again when Mattie was born, five years later. She took comfort in the old man's constancy. She loved the gentleness of his sonorous voice as he spoke the prayers of the Mass. He was a constant in a world that could be full of troubles and fluctuating fortunes, and his dispensations were soothing.

Father Robert had travelled from France and the Benedictine abbey there to join the community of the Cistercians at Vaudey, citing his wish to live a life of greater austerity, one more closely observing the Benedictine rule. The elderly monk believed strongly in self-sustenance and charity. This new Order also supported themselves through discoveries of technology in agriculture and promoting the beauty of architecture.

When Agnes had asked Father Robert why he wore robes of undyed sheep's wool rather than the black robes about which she had heard, he had explained that, while white robes had previously been worn by hermits who followed the 'angelic' life, now they represented the purity of his life in the Cistercian Order. This was of great interest to Agnes, and Clémence remembered that many questions had followed. What was the 'angelic' life of a hermit? Who might undertake that, and why? How did such a person survive?

Father Robert's voice interrupted Clémence's recollections as he removed his hand from her head. She looked up at him, wishing that she had concentrated better on his blessing.

"I have come to tell you something," he said.

"Oh?"

"I shared my news with your family before you arrived. I am leaving you and the life I have known here."

Clémence's hand flew to her mouth as she gasped.

"It will be a change for us all. I came here many years ago and baptised your sister the day I buried her mother. She was a tiny little thing, so I wrapped her in a piece of woollen cloth cut from an old habit. Later, when your father remarried, Goodwife Masson took her in as one of her own. God praise thee." He glanced across the room at Catherine and Agnes. Clémence saw her sister gazing in adoration at Father Robert. "Under my instruction and, I hope, my guidance, you girls have grown in wisdom and charity, and Mattie has loving care from you all."

"And I thank you for it, Father." Merek had entered the house and heard the last of the story.

Father Robert made to stand, but Merek waved him back into his seat. "You spent much time giving Agnes instruction and tuition, and she has become deeply devout. Our family has much to thank you for, and for which to thank God."

"Amen," Father Robert said.

"Your ministries have continued with my wife during her confinement, and with Clémmie with her learning. You will be much missed, Father."

"But how will we manage without you?" Agnes said. She was close to tears.

Father Robert chuckled. "Do not fear, child. I have a replacement. Father Deodonatus is recently come from the Mother House in Yorkshire. He is young but full of enthusiasm, and he will serve this community well, I am sure." The monk smiled. "His name means 'gift from God', so all will be well."

With those reassurances, the old man got slowly to his feet. He looked around at the family. "God go with you all," he said.

"And with you, Father." Clémence and Merek followed him to the door and watched as he shuffled away.

After he had gone, Clémence felt bereft. Her appreciation for nature was due to Father Robert. An image of them bending together to look closely at blades of grass spiked with hoar frost came to mind; watching a bee as it buzzed between blackthorn blossoms; learning the names of the trees and looking at the patterns on their leaves. All these things had helped her to understand the turning of the seasons and to appreciate each one despite the different circumstances they could bring: disease in the summer, unbearable cold in the winter. Father Robert had shown her the stars, encouraging her to identify their patterns. He had spoken with her about plants and how to utilise them for curing ills. Tales from his travels had intrigued her, too. Yes, she would miss him and his wisdom.

It wasn't until Clémence was in bed that night that she retrieved the piece of carved wood that Ruadhán had given her at the manor house. She marvelled at the skill in the flickering candlelight. It was carved into the shape of a leaf from the rowan tree for which he was named, with a tiny cluster of berries at its base. Gently she fingered the delicate veins he had carved. She would treasure it, but why had he given it to her?

CHAPTER 4

The harvest was either a time of celebration for success or fear of starvation to come. This year it was the former. For the people of Folkingham and Grimsthorpe, celebrations steeped in customs and superstitions once the back-breaking work was complete, were welcome. The first harvest of animal feeds for the winter coincided with the summer solstice, and this year the St John's Day feast had been spectacular. The villagers had burned the bones of animals on the massive 'bone fire'. The pungent aroma would ward off evil spirits and dragons. Since none appeared, there was proof that it was successful, and revelling and drinking ensued. Boys rolled the fired cartwheel down the hill to prevent the sun from turning back after reaching its highest point, and some of the braver lads jumped the embers to bring good luck.

It was on the last day of September when reaping was complete that the final celebration took place. At five in the morning the men formed a circle around the last sheaf and then threw their scythes and sickles at the base of the stalks, until they were all severed. As the last man to cut it was impossible to identify, no bad luck would result for any one of them.

Daniel presented some stalks to Agnes. "Here. For the making of a corn maiden," he said.

She thanked him graciously. "I shall honour the maiden of the corn." She turned to her sister. "Come, Clémmie, we must make haste. I'll help you make the bread so you have something to take to the festival tonight. You must not go empty-handed," Agnes said.

"You will come, though?" Clémence asked her sister with a frown.

"I think I shall give the revelling a miss. I am still upset by what happened in the woods."

"But that was weeks ago, and you know the fellow is no longer with us." Clémence crossed herself.

"I know that. I'll come to St Michael's Mass, but I'm uneasy when the drink starts to flow — the dancing and merriment seems so loud."

"Sir Ruadhán will provide goose meat, I'm certain. You won't want to miss that, surely?" Surprise made Clémence's words louder than she intended. "There will be games and stalls."

"I want no ribbons or suchlike. I shall be content. I shall come to the church, of course, and see all the autumn decorations, then I shall slip away home. Mother shall accompany me, for she is already tired."

Clémence nodded and said no more. She herself was looking forward to the evening. There may even be mummers, and she enjoyed the dancing. Perhaps the young lord would even ask her to dance. It was traditional for status to be deferred for the evening of the *Horkey* festival.

All tasks completed and the visit to the church made, Catherine and Agnes returned home, while Clémence and the rest of her family made their way excitedly to the fields around the manor house.

Trestle tables had been set up, the wooden planks weighed down by the feast, to which Clémence added their loaves, jellies and conserves. Stalls decorated with leaves and berries were selling all manner of colourful ribbons and trinkets to tempt the villagers. A band of musicians wandered through the crowd, playing cheerful tunes on a hurdy-gurdy, a vielle, a shawm and some whistles of different lengths. A platform of boards covered the grass for the dancing. It was difficult to know which way to look first. It was all so much bigger and louder than the Lammas festival, two months before, when the apple harvest was underway and loaves of bread blessed.

Clémence looked around. So many sights, so much to savour. There, the warmth of the fire, as a young boy turned the pig on its spit, the fat dripping and sizzling, causing flames to spark higher; the colours of the stalls selling bonnets and little carved toys for the younger children. There were food stalls, too, with samples to tempt customers to buy jams and conserves, dried meats or fruit. Even a knife-sharpener had arrived, and as his foot worked the treadle, sparks of yellow and silver flew from his wheel as he held a blade against it.

Daniel approached her through the crowd. "I hoped I might dance with your sister," he said.

"Agnes has gone home with my mother. She does not much care for dancing and games."

Before Daniel could respond, a roar erupted. Clémence stood on tiptoe to see what all the commotion was about.

Sir Ruadhán, stripped to the waste and hair tied high on his scalp, had begun to wrestle with Thomas Smith from the forge. The flickering torches surrounding the ring in which they struggled, shoulder to shoulder, accentuated contours and muscles beneath the flesh. Clémence saw a long scar down the knight's left side, where he had received a wound, now healed. There were murmurs as one opponent got the better of the other. What would happen if Thomas beat their lord? As yet the limit of his temper was unknown. He had been away for many years, learning techniques needed in battle, and those expected of a knight, and then fighting for de Beaumont in the north. The two men were finely matched, their right arms strengthened from swinging the tools of their respective crafts. Then, with unexpected swiftness and dexterity, Thomas floored their master. There was a moment of silence. How would Ruadhán react? After a moment, he stretched out his hand to Thomas, who pulled him upright. As he rose, he laughed with a deep-throated guffaw, slapped his opponent on the shoulder, and the whole company cheered and clapped in relief.

Clémence watched, mesmerised, as Ruadhán walked across to a laver of water and splashed his face, before throwing himself into a chair next to his uncle, who slouched in his own, a goblet in his hand. Ruadhán's eyes roamed the company and alighted upon Clémence, who quickly turned her head away, embarrassed to have been caught staring. At that moment, the band struck up and people took to the boards to dance. Daniel took her hand to make a claim, and she went with him. She knew this dance of old and as she twirled with Daniel and moved on down the line to take the hand of the next man before spinning again, she was surprised to see that it was Ruadhán, now with his shirt on. As he took her hand, he looked down at her with a smile and a flash of mirth in his blue eyes. He spun her under his arm and when the time came to place his arm around her waist, she was deeply aware of the motion of her hips swaying below his hand in time with the music. All too soon she had moved on, and she lost track of him as the dance ended.

Lost for breath, Clémence moved to the edge of the crowd. She looked around for Ruadhán, but there was no sign of him. Instead, her eyes met those of Aedric, still slouched in his chair. He smiled at her lasciviously. Shocked, Clémence turned away and found Daniel by her side.

"It seems your sister Agnes prefers the cloister, Clémmie. Why does she not become a nun? She might as well, for she is very pious."

"I believe she would if it were not for the lack of a dowry. Anyway, Agnes is needed at home. Her spinning is much finer than mine and when the new baby arrives, Mother will need our help."

"The time will come for you to wed, Clémmie. In truth, it has come already. If your sister is not of a mind, then perhaps we should consider it," he said, catching her hand and turning her to face him.

"Daniel! There are many tasks awaiting me at home, too. In fact, I must go there now." Clémence darted away to find her father and Mattie.

Having broken their fast with bread and goats' milk and ale, the Masson family commenced the day's work. Merek was already away visiting the abbey with his plans for the extension to the wool house. Mattie accompanied him, and the women had much to do preparing food for winter storage and spinning. Agnes sat with her loom by the front door, where she could admire the dawn, while Clémence planned to pickle some vegetables in salt brine and lay them in earthenware crocks. Her father had killed a goose two days before and she was to cut the confits of meat and lay them to cure in the rich fat. Once sealed in pots, this would see them through the winter.

As Clémence laid her knife on the table and went to fetch the crocks from the shelf, she heard the wheels of a cart outside.

"It's Father Robert," Agnes called. "He is leaving."

Clémence ran to the open door and watched as the cart came to a stop outside the cottage. Seated on a bench next to a lay brother was the old monk. "Today I am returning to the Mother House. It is time for me to go and live out my days in solitude."

Catherine had joined her daughters. "We wish you peace, Father," she said.

"It has been a blessing to have guarded the souls of my parishioners for so many years."

Agnes pulled the distaff holding the carded wool from her belt and cast her spindle onto the stool she vacated. She fell to her knees beside the cart and looked up at Father Robert with tears on her cheeks and her hands clasped.

The old man looked down at her with a gentle smile. "Do not weep, child. Go to church and talk to God. He will keep you and heal all ills." His gaze swept up to Clémence standing by the door. "It has been my joy to teach you, Clémmie. You have soaked up all the knowledge I could give you and your command of reading and writing will be a help to your family." He looked down again at Agnes. "Father Deodonatus will hear your confessions and help you with your Bible studies, Agnes."

Father Robert made the sign of the cross. "*Per Jesum Christum Dominum Nostrum,*" he said, and with a nod to the lay brother, the cart rumbled on its way.

Agnes turned to look at Catherine. "Mother, may I go to the church? I would like to pray in the silence there."

"Yes, of course, Agnes. Clémmie shall go with you."

Clémence looked at her mother. "I have all the vegetables to prepare and I plan to make the comfits from the goose."

"I shall make a start on that. It will serve you better to accompany your sister and when you return, you may complete the tasks." Clémence knew better than to argue, and besides, she knew that she did not go to church often enough.

The sisters crossed the narrow wooden bridge over the River Glen and Clémence looked down into the water. The river wasn't deep and sunlight danced in the ripples. Willow branches trailed their fingers in the water and some ducks quacked in the tree's shade. They stopped and crossed themselves before the statue of St Michael before entering the church through the gabled porch with its floriated buttresses. Always craving knowledge, she had learned from her father, when she was quite small, that the ashlar stones were of the best quality and fulfilled Vitruvius' three attributes of strength, utility, and beauty. A hush descended upon them as the thick stone walls wrapped them in coolness. Their Anglo-Saxon ancestors had built here originally, but now, with a population of nearly five hundred, the village and surrounding hamlets used this enlarged church regularly.

Clémence watched in silence as Agnes took to her knees and moved up the aisle thus, as her penance, though of what sins she could possibly be guilty, Clémence knew not. Her sister was devout in the extreme, still wearing her hair belt.

It was dark in the back corner, but Clémence soon realised she was not alone. A tall man, skeletally thin, had entered in silence through the west door and stood like a statue, clothed in the greyish-white of Cistercian robes, the top of his head shaved. He watched, transfixed, as Agnes moved slowly towards the altar rail with her hands clasped and her lips moving in silent entreaty to God her saviour. As she reached her goal, Agnes' voice rose to the cross on the wall as she continued to pray.

"God Almighty, who can see into my soul, who knows I have known no man, but who knowest also that I wish such wicked desires as I see all around me. Help me to resist temptation."

Wicked desires? What or who has set Agnes' heart on fire? Surely *she* should be the one praying thus, thought Clémence to herself, as the memory of Sir Ruadhán at the festival, his skin slick with sweat, crept into her mind.

She saw the curve of a small smile from the monk and it disturbed her. Clémence cleared her throat to announce her presence. Was this Father Deodonatus, who had recently arrived to replace Father Robert?

The monk spun round. "Who's there?" He must have decided he sounded too harsh for he added, more softly, "May I be of assistance?"

"Forgive me, Father. I didn't hear you enter." She nodded towards the shadows of the building, before dipping in a curtsey to the priest before her. "My sister is currently praying."

Agnes had stood at the sound of voices, and now returned down the aisle to join her sister.

The young monk turned to her. "Would you like me to hear your confession, my daughter?"

"Perhaps at the early morning prayers tomorrow. We must return to help my mother — she is near her time and must not stand for too long. There are many tasks in the home."

"Perhaps I shall visit your house," said the young monk. "Where are you from?"

"We are the daughters of Master Merek Masson."

"Ah, the mason who works on the abbey. He is going to extend the wool house, I understand, and do some carvings too."

"Yes, Father. Forgive us, we must go." Clémence was anxious to be away. This man made her feel comfortable. His skull-like face was so unlike the round, friendly face of Father Robert, but her sister tarried.

"I look forward to my confession with you. I'm sorry we must go now." Agnes bowed her head to receive the blessing of Father Deodonatus.

The air outside was refreshing and Clémence took a deep lungful. The atmosphere inside the church had changed from peaceful calm to something that she couldn't quite discern, but she hadn't like it. Now she looked up at the sky, felt the breeze upon her face and listened to the rustling of the leaves on the beech trees. She took another deep breath. The seasons turned with predictability and all would be well.

CHAPTER 5

Agnes returned to the church the following day, but Clémence claimed she was too busy with her domestic responsibilities. "I was absent for much of yesterday and now I must catch up," she said. "There are still the comfits of goose to finish layering in the fat and I must finish salting the carrots or we shall go hungry when the weather turns. You can take your distaff and spindle with you and spin as you walk, but I am unable to undertake my tasks unless I remain here." With that she watched as Agnes tidied her hair, replaced her scarf, and left the house.

"Piety is important to your sister, Clémmie," their mother said as she sat at the doorway, spinning. "I shall work on this fleece while she is away. Then there is some flax to spin, and the weaving, too. The new baby will need cloths aplenty."

"How are you feeling, Mother?" Clémence asked.

"I shall be pleased when this one is born. It has been kicking all week."

"It will surely be soon then."

"It will. You may have to run for Goodwife Carpenter at any moment."

Sunday came and Clémence could put off a visit to the church no longer. There was an even greater turnout than usual for the service. Most of the villagers had seen Father Robert depart and were curious to meet the new priest. There was already a crush of people when the Masson family entered the building.

There would be no courtiers here. The de Beaumonts, if at home, would attend in their own castle chapel, but the local nobility, seated above her head in the gallery, would all be here today, Clémence was certain.

As the villagers stood crowded together, Clémence looked around at the colourful images on the walls. The pictures told the stories from the Bible. There was a Doom painting on the chancel, placed for all to see. It was 'The Last Judgement', with the Virgin Mary on Christ's right and St John the Baptist on Christ's left. There was a colourful picture of the miracle of Jesus raising Lazarus, and another of Archangel Michael with his trumpet. She would understand the words and stories the priest was to speak in Latin, but few around her would.

Clémence had fixed a sprig of rosemary for remembrance to her collar and as she caught the scent, she thought of her two dead sisters, who had not survived for many months and who now lay in the graveyard outside. She prayed silently for her mother's confinement to come. She thought too of Father Robert, and was grateful for the opportunities of learning he had given to her. Agnes had relished Bible tuition, but she had enjoyed reading and writing, as well as learning about the natural world.

Clémence glanced up and behind, to the gallery. Was that a fiery head of hair below a purple cap? She averted her eyes with haste, and looked around at the ceiling with its beams and carved angels, pretending she hadn't been looking for Ruadhán.

A hush descended and Clémence saw that Father Deodonatus had entered from the vestry with his attendants. For the next fifteen minutes or so, she tried hard to listen, but she was distracted by thoughts of Ruadhán, the rustle of clothing and feet on the stone floor, and the coughing of an elderly man.

Father Deodonatus' voice rose in an impassioned plea to the Almighty to curse all sinners. "Repent or your soul will forever burn in Hell," he said. "You will feel His wrath…" How different this was to Father Robert's gentle, if somewhat rambling sermons. Although the message might be similar, the old priest's delivery denoted a God who was benevolent and forgiving, unlike Father Deodonatus' God, who would forever damn those who strayed from the path of righteousness.

Then came time to receive the body and blood of Christ. Clémence shuffled forward and knelt at the altar rail with the rest. She shrank from Father Deodonatus' long, bony fingers as he passed the cup to her. His tongue flicked out onto his top lip as he moved in front of Agnes.

After, they all emerged into the full light of the morning. There was lively chatter as people exchanged news, children swooping in and out of the crowd, chasing each other whilst parents scolded them. Daniel was there, talking with a group of other young men. He didn't approach Clémence or her family, but cast frequent glances in their direction.

One conversation in particular drew Clémence's attention. "She's coming to visit the manor, apparently." It was Thomas from the forge. He was speaking with Daniel's father, William, who was also a *sokeman*.

"How do you know that?"

"I was at the forge shoeing a horse. The rider told me. He said that Lady Emma was coming in a few weeks and that she'll stay with one of her own women at the manor. Before Sir Ruadhán's father passed away —" Thomas crossed himself — "an arrangement was made between the two families."

Clémence's heart was thumping. A young woman was coming to the manor. Were she and Ruadhán betrothed? She edged closer to William that she might better hear, but the conversation had turned and she became no wiser. *An arrangement was made between the two families.* This young woman — Lady Emma — must be bringing a good dowry.

Clémence was filled with a feeling of disappointment. She and the young knight were from vastly different stations in society, even if her own father was a master mason and much respected. Her daydreams of the two of them together were nothing but a ridiculous fancy. Ruadhán would marry for wealth, and maybe even for love.

Clémence wanted to go home. She pulled her shawl tighter around her shoulders. "Father, should we not go soon? Mother will be tiring."

"Yes, child. You, Agnes and Mattie may go with your mother, and I shall follow shortly. I want to talk with Master Farmer here, about borrowing his new plough. I hear Master Smith has just affixed a new iron coulter. It'll cut through our heavy clay soil so much better. And we have other things to discuss," he added, without further explanation.

Clémence was uneasy at this last remark and hoped it didn't involve any future with Daniel. She was aware that she couldn't evade a betrothal to someone for much longer, even if it was not what she wanted.

At that moment, Daniel approached. "Perhaps I might walk with you, Clémmie. It's been a while since we last spoke."

"By all means, Daniel. We are just leaving now. Father will be pleased to see you escorting us."

Daniel's shoulders slumped and Clémence had the grace to feel sorry for him.

"I meant me and you. I didn't realise all your family were leaving also."

"We may follow on behind. It's of no matter." As others drifted away from the church and started the trek to their respective dwellings, Clémence's family did the same and Daniel walked at her side. They said nothing for several minutes, until Clémence could stand the silence no longer. "I thought you wanted to speak with me, Daniel?"

He nodded and cleared his throat. "If Agnes is so determined not to wed, 'tis high time we talked about the possibility, Clémmie. You're seventeen and I'm eighteen years, nearly nineteen."

"Perhaps, but all is far from settled, Daniel. Our fathers may be discussing possibilities but there is no agreement as yet." Clémence sighed. This was far from the romantic proposal she craved. It was only recently that Daniel had been hankering after her sister. She wanted to be second fiddle in his choice even less.

They walked on in silence, before Daniel broke it. "Father sub-enfeoffed the fields of Madoc Oswyne after his passing. Sir Aedric wanted to keep the land himself for the demesne, but in the end he agreed. Father had to pay an inflated rate — four pennies an acre, but the extra crops will more than make up for that. Our yields are back up to three bushels of grain per hectare now, after the Great Famine, and the beans and lentils are doing better."

Although the Great Famine had been nearly ten years ago, Clémence remembered it well. Many people had died because there was little food to go round, though she never did take to the taste of ground acorns to make the food go further. Praise God her family had survived. She made the sign of the cross. "I don't know what people did to bring down His wrath like that."

"Me neither, but the rain was never-ending. We thought another great flood might be coming. They say rain like that comes every ten or twelve years."

"Pray to God you are wrong," Clémence said.

"What I am trying to say is that my father is well placed and so I shall be — to support a family, I mean."

This was far from the romantic notions Clémence craved and she was sure that Sir Ruadhán would not woo his bride in that manner, although he probably had not proposed at all, but listened to the terms of an arrangement made on his behalf many years ago. Then she chided herself. To think of the lord of the manor in this way was not her concern, though the unfairness of it still rankled. She could see where the conversation was leading. "You better be getting along, Daniel. With extra land to plough now the harvest is in, your father will need you."

"We've completed the first pull, so all the stubble's turned in."

"Still, there will be the thistles and other weeds to see to with the next pass."

"Yes, but there's plenty of time before that and the third pass, when we'll sow the winter varieties. Clémmie, I —"

"Well, you may have time to spare, but I have spinning to do," she cut in. "If we are to have cloth for winter we must make haste. It's a never-ending task, as you know. There are crab apples to pick as well. Mattie will climb and shake the tree, but he's the only one who will do that part."

Daniel jumped at the idea. "I can come and help with that. If Mattie and I both shake the bows, you and Agnes can hold the sack sheets underneath. Perhaps your mother might help? She need not be bending to pick the windfalls."

Clémence realised she had given him an opportunity and mentally chastised herself. She sighed. "Very well. I'll see you later after we have changed from our Sunday clothing."

As they worked, Clémence looked up at Daniel in the tree as his eyes flicked between Agnes and herself. *He's like a sick goat*, she thought, *but I'll not marry him, not even to please Father.* She glanced at her sister, holding the other end of the sacking sheet. *I could go into a nunnery with Agnes.* Then she smiled at the idea, for she knew she was incapable of leading a life of self-abnegation. Anyway, there was insufficient money for one dowry, never mind two at the rates the nunnery would expect at Sleaford, or even Stixwould.

As she continued with her task, Clémence's thoughts wandered. As a *sokeman*, her father paid one stook of corn in ten for his rent, while taxes were either nearly half of what he earned, or hours spent working on the manor lands. He had little time to spare, working as a mason, so he had to give crops or money. A dowry to a nunnery was out of the question.

They had heard the bell for Vespers, which rang an hour earlier on a Sunday than the rest of the week, but they continued with their work. It could not stop, not for them, nor any of the other villagers. The cattle still needed milking, hens fed and pigs in the woods checked for good health. They saw the band of monks as they took their evening walk, chanting silently with hands hidden in sleeves. The sun hung motionless on the horizon, casting a golden glow on their pale habits.

Finally they heard the bell for Compline, the signal for work to stop at last, and to consume some supper before the balm of sleep.

Daniel bid farewell, a sullen expression reflecting his disappointment at being unable to speak with Merek regarding a betrothal to Clémence.

The family sat around the table, Merek at the head. He scooped up bacon and peas with a knife from his own platter, using a thick slice of corn bread to soak up the dripping. Mattie had a similar plate as he sat on the bench along one side and the two sisters shared a wooden plate opposite. Catherine sat next to her son, after she had served her husband. Food was plentiful in the autumn months, and cheese with a spoonful or two of blackberry jelly awaited them.

Suddenly, the family heard the sound of horse's hooves and a rider reined to a halt outside the cottage. They all stopped eating in surprise and looked at one another. It was late for a messenger. Mattie grabbed Catherine's skirt in customary agitation.

"Fear not, Mattie," said Merek, "it is James atte Wode. I know his father, Stephen."

Merek rose, and Clémence moved to stand beside her mother, who had struggled to her feet, clutching her swollen stomach. Agnes went to calm her brother. The rider had already dismounted and was approaching. They could see from the colours of the livery under the saddle that he had come from Amundeville's manor.

The man addressed Merek. "Apologies for disturbing you, Master. A word with you, if you will."

"Come inside, James. Is something amiss?"

"Not that I know." He seated himself on the end of the bench and accepted the mug of ale that Clémence placed before him. "I have a message for ye, though. There are orders from your sister Joan, the housekeeper, but they come from my lord. You're to bring your daughter to the manor at first light, fit and ready to start work there."

"What's this? Agnes is to start work at the manor house? She has many accomplishments in household arts, of course, but would have no wish for life in the manor." Merek was indignant. "She is a God-fearing young woman and would not do well in such society."

"Not Mistress Agnes, sir. Mistress Clémence here." He nodded towards Clémence. "Sir Ruadhán's bride-to-be, Lady Emma, has arrived and her woman has taken sick." He looked at their aghast expressions. Sickness was something about which to be concerned. "Oh, it's nothing for you to worry about. The maid is with child and has been sent back to her family. Sir Aedric will not maintain her keep."

"Clémence is to go?" said Catherine. "But how will we manage?" Worry etched itself on her mother's face. "It's hard enough with both girls here, and soon there will be another to care for and feed."

"We shall make the best of it," replied Merek. "If our daughter is to serve the young lady, then it is an honour indeed."

"She is to serve as maid and companion," James said. "The young mistress is not far from your daughter in age. It won't be long until the handfasting, and then my Lady Emma and Sir Ruadhán will get to know each other better before the nuptials. Shall I return to the manor and tell them you will arrive shortly after first light?"

Clémence stood in silence, not trusting her voice to speak without a tremor. How would she cope seeing Ruadhán each day, and with his nuptials so close? Should she refuse? It was, however, an opportunity to achieve what her heart craved, to be part of a bigger world.

Everyone was waiting to hear her decision. She made up her mind and spoke. "I am honoured. Please convey my thanks for this great consideration. Father? I see I must go."

"But we've had no chance to see to your clothing or to … to prepare you," said Catherine. "You have no notion of being a lady's maid, never mind a companion."

"Hush, Wife. All will be well," said Merek. "This is an opportunity for Clémmie."

James stood to take his leave. "There's no call for Clémence to bring much. Goodwife Joan will provide all that is necessary and teach her aught she needs to know."

Mattie started rocking, upset with all the commotion and understanding little. Agnes put her arm around his shoulders and Clémence gently soothed him.

Merek closed the door after the messenger, and turned to Clémence. "Go and gather what you might want to take with you."

Clémence grabbed a basket hanging in the corner and rushed up the steps to the loft.

"Mattie, fetch the cheese from the cold slab in the larder. Agnes, go and help your sister and then return with all speed. We shall finish the meal we started."

His tone had the desired effect upon each of them and slowly order was restored.

That night, as Clémence and Agnes lay beside each other, sleep would come to neither. Mattie lay on his back, his breath coming in regular gentle puffs.

"Mattie will be fine once I'm gone," Clémence whispered into the dark.

"I know," answered Agnes. "If given clear instructions, he'll be able to do some work around here in the evenings after his day with Father. He needs more occupation anyway. It's just that … I'll miss you, Clémmie. I know it's an opportunity for you, but I shall worry nonetheless. Take care of yourself, won't you?"

"I shall, dear sister. And I'll come back to see you all when Mother has the baby."

Beside her, Agnes gave a long sigh.

Clémence closed her eyes and fell into a deep sleep.

CHAPTER 6

Clémence stirred at the sound of the abbey bells calling the monks to Vigils, before drifting back into an uneasy sleep. Inevitably, early morning light came creeping into the cottage through the shutters' and the family all stirred. By the time the bells for Lauds chimed, Clémence was dressed and called down to her mother to ask if she might bind her hair in a fillet, as she had seen the gentry wear.

She had dressed with care and used the comb her father had carved for her, before placing it in the basket and hurrying down the steps from the loft. The family had dressed and were breaking their fast.

Clémence glanced at each of them in turn. Catherine looked worried, Agnes low-spirited, even Merek was anxious. Only Mattie looked his usual self, casually unaware of what was to come. Clémence herself was nervous with anticipation, despite her lack of sleep.

Merek cracked the shutters open as dawn light gave way to early morn, allowing Catherine to extinguish precious candles. A cockerel gave voice as a breeze freshened the air in the household, indicating that it was time to go if they were to arrive after first light.

"Mind your manners, now," said Catherine, "and be polite to your Aunt Joan, too. She holds a position of some importance and I do not want her to think I have not raised you properly."

"Yes, Mother," Clémence answered meekly. She knew her mother's brusqueness was due to her concern.

"At least you're able to turn a fine seam. You'll be expected to care for the young lady's garments."

"I'll do my best, Mother. You will send word when the babe is born?"

Catherine nodded and reached out to smooth Clémence's hair. "There, child, you had best be going. God bless you," she said in softened tones.

Agnes came forward. "God speed, sister. We shall all miss you."

Clémence gave her sister an impetuous hug. She was leaving all that was familiar.

The cloudy skies promised rain, but Clémence refused to let it dampen her spirits. As they walked, Marek carried her basket in one hand and a sack bag on his shoulder. She knew not what the bag contained for it was all sharp corners and edges, but supposed it was something to deliver to his sister.

As they walked through the woods, the early morning breeze caused the branches to creak. There was rustling amongst the dense undergrowth. Reminded of her recent altercation with the homeless ruffian, Clémence pulled her broadcloth shawl closer around her shoulders, and slipped her arm through her father's.

"Don't be afraid, lass. There's nothing to be frightened of with me at your side," Marek said, quietly reassuring. "The small animals of the night will be creeping away to find a place to sleep, that's all."

As they left the woods and crossed the fields on the rough track, there was little to say and Clémence was left to her own thoughts. She remembered all the journeys she had made with her father as a young child, accompanying him nearly everywhere despite Catherine's disapproval. She had learned patience, but so much more besides, when talking with him about his travels. She also wondered who had suggested that she be chosen to accompany Lady Emma. Perhaps it was Aunt

Joan, but then she dismissed that idea. Agnes would be her preferred choice. Perhaps it was Sir Ruadhán himself. Heat rose to her cheeks at the thought. She would be at the centre of manor life and would certainly see him most days. Her expectation increased as they crossed the gently undulating land towards the manor house.

Crossing the wooden bridge over the moat, Clémence looked up. Like the abbey, the church, and King John's Tower, ashlar blocks carved from a local quarry ensured the building was sturdy. Fortified as it was, it would withstand arrows and axes, and possibly even the small cannons that Father Robert had told her had begun to appear in Europe at the beginning of their young king's reign. Passing once more through the small door set into the massive gates, as they had done previously, Merek and Clémence crossed the courtyard and made their way to the great hall. Inside, straw-filled pallets were stacked up against one wall and with the morning meal finished, two servants were in the process of putting trestle tables to one side.

Sitting before the fire in a huge carved chair sat Sir Aedric Amundeville. His feet rested on a footstool and he guffawed loudly at some badinage from the men around him. He raised his tankard and took a deep draft, letting some of the contents dribble down his beard before he wiped it away with the cuff of his woollen cotehardie. Catching site of the newcomers, he waved his tankard and shouted across to them. "Ha! The mason and his daughter. Come forward. I see you have followed my instruction with proper speed."

His instruction. Sir Aedric's command has brought me here. Clémence's hope that Ruadhán may have been behind the order were crushed with that one sentence.

Merek placed a hand upon her shoulder as they moved forward and she was grateful for its reassuring pressure. Aedric made no move, but stared up at them blearily. Perhaps it was wine in his mug and not ale, even at this early hour.

"How now, Mason, still carving your Godly masterpieces?" Some of his companions sniggered.

"I must thank you, sir, for your timely intervention on behalf of my daughters recently." When Aedric looked blank, Merek added, "In the woods."

"Eh? Oh, yes, indeed. Just in time, too. Almost lost their maidenheads, both of them." He grinned at Clémence and belched quietly.

Ruadhán stopped at the top of the stairs. He recognised the young woman he had rescued in the woods not so long ago, as she edged forwards to stand beside her father in front of Aedric.

The image of her laughing as they danced at the *Horkey* festival flitted through his memory. Curls of hair, the colour of autumn leaves, had worked their way free from her coif and he recalled the way her hazel eyes had reflected the firelight as she twirled lightly on her feet.

"A fine-looking girl, this daughter of yours, Mason," said Aedric now as he scratched his beard.

"She's a modest, good girl," Merek said, "and soon to be wed."

Clémence glanced up at her father. Perhaps he was saying that to protect her from this powerful man.

Aedric guffawed before shouting for his nephew.

Clémence heard footsteps on the stairs at the far end of the hall. When she turned, she saw Sir Ruadhán striding across towards them.

He nodded at the newcomers before halting in front of them. "What brings you here, Master Masson?" Ruadhán spared a glance for Clémence and despite herself, her heart began to thump.

"I understood you requested that I bring my daughter to wait upon your young guest, the Lady Emma. Now we have arrived, early as instructed, I discover it was not your bidding, my lord, but that of your uncle, Sir Aedric."

Aedric raised his beaker. "It seemed a fitting appointment, under the circumstances. I'm certain Lady Emma will benefit from having a companion to attend her. And I'm sure we shall all enjoy seeing her here too," he added.

Ruadhán ignored his uncle. "It's true Emma needs a new companion during her stay here. She will need someone to help her now that her maid has left." He turned to Clémence. "Your aunt is housekeeper here, I believe?"

Clémence dropped a small curtsey. "Yes, sir."

Ruadhán nodded. "Go through to the kitchens. Joan will find you some suitable clothing and will take you to Lady Emma's room, where you can become acquainted."

Merek bowed his head and Clémence bobbed another curtsey before heading for the doorway beside the great fireplace.

"See you later," Aedric called after them as Clémence scurried after her father.

As Ruadhán watched them leave, his uncle spoke. "I see by the look on your face that you like the young maid."

"Nonsense, Uncle. Emma and I are to be handfasted and we shall wed in the fullness of time, as my father and hers wished."

"All the more for me, then." Aedric slurped from his tankard and his friends chortled.

"Get out, the lot of you!" Ruadhán shouted, angered by his uncle's words. "We have business to discuss here." Ruadhán waved his arm and the men retreated outside, towards the stable.

"What ho, Nephew?"

"I have news from Nottingham. A messenger arrived early this morning, well before the Lauds bell. He rode first to Folkingham to deliver the news to my Lord de Beaumont and his household."

"Oh? What deserves such haste?"

"The trouble between France and England continues. King Edward has not forgiven the French kings for the encouragement they gave to the Scots for their attacks upon us."

"Edward already hates Philip. They may be cousins but Edward should have been king, since he is nephew to the late French king, not Philip," Aedric said. "Edward declaring himself King of France last year has done little for his cause, and angered Philip even more." Aedric raised his cup and quaffed deeply.

"Exactly! Adding the fleur-de-lys to his coat of arms doesn't make Edward any more King of France than it did before."

"Have a care what you say, Nephew."

"Our king knows I am loyal. I have the wounds to prove it." Ruadhán touched his side and Aedric scowled. "In addition, allying himself in Brittany with John de Montfort rather than Charles of Blois has further riled the situation. King Philip wants to see his nephew Charles installed as Duke of Brittany. My informant tells me that Charles has finally taken Nantes. He had a strong French and Breton army and now John de Montfort is a prisoner."

"And what of John's wife? Joan of Flanders is a redoubtable woman."

"She continues the fight in her husband's name, but has withdrawn to the southwest, a town named Hennebont. If taken, the chances are she will call upon King Edward for assistance."

"Then you'll be back in the fray, Nephew?"

"Quite possibly."

"Thank the Lord I am too old to fight. Don't worry, I'll watch over everyone here in your absence, again."

The door to the kitchens opened, distracting Ruadhán from responding.

Joan led Merek and Clémence across the hall towards the stairs at the far end. Clémence was suddenly nervous, and as her father wished her well and prepared to depart, she clasped his hand.

He leaned towards her. "Fear not, child. Before I depart, I shall speak with Sir Ruadhán and inform him of your betrothal. He is honour-bound to protect you in all things."

"But I am not betrothed yet," Clémence said, puzzled.

"Indeed, Daughter, but the notion will be your armour. In the meantime, heed your mother's advice and be good."

"I shall, Father. Thank you."

"God keep and bless you." He kissed her forehead. "I have a gift for you. He opened his bag and withdrew a wooden box he had been working on. The copper lid, which glowed in the dim light of the great hall, was affixed to the wooden base with ornate hinges.

"The copper is strong and will be resistant to moisture. It will last many years."

"It's so beautiful." Clémence could not resist stroking the smooth wood. "Thank you, Father. I shall treasure it."

As he turned away, tears stung her eyes as she climbed the stairs behind her Aunt Joan to Lady Emma's chamber.

As they entered the chamber, Joan said, "Good morning, my lady. I trust you slept well. I see you have been up already and opened the shutters." The housekeeper stooped and picked up a fallen garment, folded it and placed it on the coffer at the end of the bed, before adding, "You should have better concern for your gowns, my lady." She might have been reproving a careless child.

Lady Emma lay in an enormous bed with the coverlet drawn up to her chin. Clémence notice that her eyes were red, as though she had recently shed tears.

The young woman stared at Clémence and asked, "Who is this?"

"This is my niece, Clémence Masson. Her father is a *sokeman* and master mason to Lord de Beaumont at Folkingham, as well as to the abbey on the Grimsthorpe land. Sir Aedric says she will be a good companion to you, since your own maid left. You are of similar age and I'm sure she will keep you amused."

Joan turned to Clémence. "Return to the kitchen and bring something to break Lady Emma's fast. Then fetch a bowl of water so that she may wash." She nodded at the copper-lidded box and lowered her voice. "Put that down in a corner and do as I have bid you. I have my own duties to attend. Give the lady no cause for complaint."

As Clémence left the room, she wondered if that was going to be easy. Lady Emma seemed haughty and spoilt.

When Clémence returned with a tray, Emma had not moved.

As she poured ale into a pewter cup, Emma pulled a face. "Must I drink that? I do detest it so."

"Mistress Joan says it is good for you." She bustled about, picking up expensive clothing that had been strewn across the floor and folding them as she spoke. "Perhaps later we might take a walk in the gardens. The weather is set fair."

"Maybe," Emma said, and sighed. "For now, you may sit and tell me about yourself. I was unaware that you were coming. And what's that box?"

Clémence did as bid and perched at the end of the bed. "It is a gift made by my father, for keeping my small treasures inside — not that I have anything of value."

"I did not know that Sir Ruadhán had asked for you to come. He said nothing to me."

"I understand it was Sir Aedric who sent the order, my lady."

"You must call me Emma. I am in sore need of a confidante." She looked small and sad. "It is so boring here. I had to leave my little dog and my friends." Her fingers picked at the coverlet. "I shall be glad of a friend, if we may be that."

"I'm sure that we shall," Clémence said, and smiled.

CHAPTER 7

Clémence was to sleep in the great hall along with the other servants. She was conscious of numerous pairs of eyes watching her as she retrieved a straw pallet and found a space for it on the rushes. Then she heard a voice. "Clémmie Masson, what are you doing here?"

It was Marie, the miller's daughter. Clémence had not seen her since the day she had slapped her for tormenting a young Mattie with a stinging nettle. They had avoided speaking since.

"I have been asked to companion Lady Emma while she is here for the handfasting, since her own maid had to leave."

Marie gaped at her in surprise, then her expression became closed. "Huh! Anyone could do that. Picking up after someone all the time."

"And what do you do here?" Clémence asked.

"I work in the kitchen. It's skilled and important work."

"I'm new here, too," a small voice added. Clémence turned to see a thin, fair girl with darting eyes.

Marie sniffed disdainfully. "All *she* does is scour pots in the kitchen."

Clémence glanced at the girl's hands and saw her fingers were red and sore. "What's your name?"

"Hawise Webb."

"I have some of my mother's unguent. You may have some for your hands." Clémence retrieved a small earthenware pot from her basket and passed it to the girl. "Here, you may keep it. I can get more when I visit my home."

Hawise looked at her with wide eyes, as if she was unused to receiving such gestures of kindness. Clémence watched as she headed off towards her own pallet.

Marie tutted and left also.

As Clémence lay on her pallet with her shawl over her for added warmth, she listened to the unfamiliar sounds of those around her bedding down for the night — the grunts, snores, and mutterings. On the other side of the hall, a dog scratched vigorously. The oiled linen stretched across the window openings rustled in the night-time breeze. It was all so strange, but Clémence dozed eventually.

The following night, Lady Emma demanded that Clémence slept in her chamber and had a mattress transported to the room, for which Clémence was most grateful. As they settled into a routine, Emma began to relax in her company.

Ruadhán was frequently around, but spent little time with Lady Emma. He was always chivalrous and polite, but Clémence could see no attraction between them. Emma showed no interest in him, while Clémence blushed when he was close. Ruadhán seemed to spend much of his time riding or hunting, or going to King John's Tower and its tiltyard, where the men-at-arms practised their skills.

A few weeks later, word came that Clémence's mother had given birth to a baby boy. It had been a breech birth, and Catherine was still very poorly.

Approaching Emma, Clémence said, "May I go to visit my home? I'm worried for my mother."

"What will I do while you are gone? I have need of you here."

"I shall be gone but one night and will hasten back, I promise."

"Very well. But only for one night." Emma sounded peevish.

When Clémence arrived home, she was disturbed to find her mother weak and the baby boy ailing already, when she understood he had been born strong.

"Mother has lost a lot of blood," Agnes told her.

"I will make the fennel concoction. It will help to bring in and strengthen her milk and you must give it to her each day," Clémence said. "We cannot have the babe weakening any further, not when she finally has another boy."

The time disappeared too quickly, and the next day Clémence knew she could delay no longer and must return to her post. Before she left, she kissed her mother's pale cheek and stroked the baby's face with her finger.

"Don't fret for us, my child. This is a wonderful opportunity for you. Be good, look after the young lady well, and we shall be proud of you."

"Yes, Mother."

Clémence hugged her father. To see him so careworn distressed her greatly, and she had tears in her eyes as she turned to leave.

"Let me walk a short way with you, sister," said Agnes.

Clémence was pleased for her companionship. The birds were singing among the treetops as they walked, and dappled light fell on the path ahead. They saw someone approaching.

"Oh no," said Agnes.

"What is it?" Clémence looked across, startled by the expression on her sister's face.

"It's Father Deodonatus. He is not like Father Robert at all."

"How so? I thought you enjoyed discussing the scriptures?"

It was too late for further discourse as Father Deodonatus greeted them.

"Daughters," he said. "I was on my way to see you, Agnes. It is several days since you came to church, and Mistress Clémence, it is far too long since your confession."

"I am working at the big house now, Father. I have visited the chapel there."

"Why do you not kneel, daughters?" His gaze shifted from one sister to the other and his tongue flicked across his upper lip like a snake Clémence had seen in the grass not so long ago. "Even here among God's creation you may receive my blessing."

Agnes knelt, so Clémence followed. She kept her eyes down as Father Deodonatus made the sign of the cross and began murmuring in Latin.

Then his voice rose and he spoke in English. "You, my daughter," he placed his hand upon Clémence's head, "are no longer in the shelter of your home but have come into a world where lurks Temptation and Sin and there is every chance for them to flourish. The Devil may offer you every opportunity and you are a frail female."

His hand increased its pressure on her scalp and Clémence flinched.

He dropped his arm to his side. "You are a weak and frail female given the Curse of Eve. With your wickedness and your own sinful nature, you have the ability to lure men from the path of righteousness and self-control…" Clémence could see his knuckles turning white as his fingers curled into his palms.

Her knees began to ache as he continued. From her experience, men needed no leading or encouragement into sin. The ruffian in the forest had received no encouragement.

Clémence glanced up at the priest. There were beads of sweat on his upper lip as he bent forwards towards them. She crossed herself with haste and the abrupt movement seemed to break the spell. He wiped his hand across his face. "Mistress Clémence remember what I have said to you, and you also, Mistress Agnes."

They scrambled to their feet and Agnes clasped Clémence's hand. "I'll walk a little further with you."

As spring drew near, there was enormous excitement throughout the manor as the day of the handfasting approached. Among the ladies, clothes were cleaned, mended, pressed and new ribbons purchased and affixed. Emma insisted that Clémence would have a new gown reflecting the colours of her own, more lavishly decorated dress.

The kitchens were a hive of activity. Vegetables, previously pickled, were waiting to be drenched in honey; saffron, salt and spices was poured over firm cabbage hearts and left to steep; chicken liver pâtés and other meat mortrews were prepared; fish was made ready for poaching in salted water with almonds, and meat hung in preparation for grilling and stewing. The sweetmeats and desserts included cherry pottage, cream custard tarts, and rose puddings.

The betrothal was *sponsalia de future*, whereby the young couple made a promise to marry each other at some point in the future. It was a serious and binding ceremony, at which the parents of the couple signed agreements of finance or benefit and everyone knew that marriage would follow in time. Clémence had learned this during one of her walks with Lady Emma. The weather was milder now with the onset of spring. They had crossed the moat and strolled among the field flowers.

"Will you return to your father after the ceremony?" Clémence was concerned for her own position. She may well have to go home. Whatever happened, she would not wish to stay at the manor without her young mistress.

"That was the original intention," Emma replied, "but now I understand that I am to stay until the formal marriage, though there is no date set for that yet. My home is in the Fens and the journey is dependent on the weather. Flooding is a common occurrence." She smiled and the mood lightened. "Here, the seasons are less extreme. I prefer it."

Upon their return to the manor, a lively game of hot cockles was taking place in the great hall, but Emma turned away. "I'm tired from our walk," she said. "I have a much calmer game I can share with you. It's called chess. Do you know it, Clémmie?"

"I do not."

"The Danish king, Canute, brought it to this country more than two hundred years ago. You have a quick mind and will learn the moves with speed."

Lady Emma spent the next hour teaching Clémence the names and different moves of the playing pieces. Clémence laughed at the idea of the queen being more powerful than the king, and delighted that Her Majesty could outmanoeuvre her partner.

Clémence was concentrating on her next move when she realised that Ruadhán was standing beside her.

"Don't let me disturb the game," he said, as Clémence made to rise and curtsey. "I see you are close to trapping your opponent's king."

Lady Emma avoided his gaze and said nothing.

Seeing that Emma was vexed by the comment, Clémence made a false move, enabling Emma's king to escape.

In response, Lady Emma reached across the board and knocked the piece over. "I concede. I'm bored with this game. Let us go to my room."

Aware of Ruadhán's gaze upon them as the two women retreated, Clémence risked a glance back and their eyes met. She blushed and he laughed before turning to join some friends around the fireplace.

The day of the handfasting arrived and chairs were set out in the great hall; side by side for the young couple and, facing them, seats for each member of the extended families. Clémence stood to the side, just behind her mistress's chair. Father Deodonatus would be presiding over the event. She had only seen him in the distance when he had visited the manor house, and not had cause to accept the sacrament from him since their meeting on the path that day. His flicking tongue stayed in her memory and she avoided his eyes. She knew he had visited her mother at their house several times. Word had arrived that Catherine and the baby were doing well.

Emma looked fresh in her new blue gown with ribbons at her shoulders and her hair fastened under a hood of white. A few stray blonde curls escaped prettily. Ruadhán stood with fortitude as Sir Aedric, in the absence of Ruadhán's father, wrapped a plaited crimson and blue ribbon to represent each of their houses around the couple's wrists, symbolically tying them together.

"I, Ruadhán Edward William Amundeville, take thee Emma…" his words faded as Clémence's thoughts wandered.

Ruadhán. An Irish name for the tree with red berries, followed by two English patriotic names, she thought. *What could be more fitting.*

Emma's voice was barely above a whisper and Clémence thought her hand shook as Ruadhán held it in his. After the completion of the vows, Aedric untied the ribbon, and gave each of the betrothed half of a gold penny, split down the centre.

The ceremony over, the elders led the young couple away to take their seats at the table for the banquet.

That night, as the two young women lay in the dark in Emma's chamber, Emma whispered, "I'm pleased to be here with you, Clémmie."

If Emma had been married fully, she would have to share a bed with her husband. Clémence was pleased, too.

CHAPTER 8

Ruadhán had been up since daybreak. He hadn't slept much anyway, in anticipation of the first land battle which was to come. Several of his comrades had congregated either at Folkingham Castle or at the manor house. William de Bohun, the first Earl of Northampton and grandson to Edward I, must have inherited his formidable fighting spirit from that king. Since the new de Beaumont was just a young boy, William was at the manor. He and Ruadhán's liege lord, the elder de Beaumont, had fought together in Scotland and learned much about warfare, especially following their defeat at Bannockburn. In fact, it was de Beaumont's suggestion to change the whole strategy. Many hours spent deliberating battle preparation meant they were well-prepared, though the forthcoming fight in France would prove to be an important test of those theories. The knights of Folkingham and Grimsthorpe were aware of developing themes from battles in which they, too, had been involved north of the border.

Ruadhán and his uncle had previously discussed the Battle of Sluys in June of 1340, and this morning was no different.

"The loss of the French fleet, as well as their allies from Castille and Genoa, will ensure we cross the Channel with ease," Ruadhán said as the two men broke their fast.

"It was a bold move from King Edward, especially since his spies, Crawley and Crabbe, advised against attack in such a confined space, even if the Flemish harbour is large."

"I heard he flew into a rage and vowed to deliver the attack immediately, ignoring their suggestion to desist."

"He certainly has a temper." Aedric took a deep quaff of his wine.

"The French ships were more manoeuvrable back then." Another knight stood with his foot on the fender in front of the fireplace.

"So how was it such a disaster for the enemy?" a much younger knight asked.

"Because they were all roped together, making manoeuvres more difficult. They couldn't turn or avoid our fire, even though they had a shallower draft." He looked up. "It was a bloodbath."

"Remember, I was there, too," another man reminded him. "No one dared tell King Philip that his fleet had been destroyed. Eventually his jester broke the news to him with a joke that softened the blow. He told him that the French knights were much braver than the English, for none of the English has dared to jump into the sea wearing full armour."

All the company laughed.

"So now, because Edward will not pay fealty and acknowledge Philip as King of the French, as his father did, we are to go to battle for him."

"Edward expressed his claim to the French throne when he quartered the royal coat of arms of England — the three lions — with that of the golden fleur-de-lys of France," Ruadhán said.

"Edward's strength is in his forward planning. To have all the merchants from the Kentish Cinque Ports on his side and ready with their cogs in return for granting trading privileges was a smart move."

Before it was fully light, the young men headed to the stables. The blacksmith's hammer had been ringing for days and the retainers, squires and attendants had been working to ensure they repaired all armour, cleaned all chainmail, and ensured all was ready again.

Ruadhán was grateful to Henry de Beaumont for giving him a new shield for services rendered on previous battlefields, before the older lord had gone to meet his maker. While he wouldn't necessarily carry it into battle, for he would need both hands on his weapons, it displayed his loyalty and he was pleased to show it off to other knights in the company. The preceding day, attendants had stowed the hooded hauberk with new leather laces attached, trousers, leather gauntlets, and shoes, all made of chainmail, in the carts. The plate armour, so valuable, would be placed in the locked coffers before the whole company departed.

Emma had fashioned a padded coat for Ruadhán, made from a double layer of linen and stuffed between with wool. When she had presented it to him, he had kissed Emma on her cheek. He had thanked Clémence for her assistance and found her gentle blush captivating. When she had turned away in haste, his attraction was complete.

As the two women retired and Ruadhán placed the new clothing on a chair, one of the young soldiers said, "I bet the fig of that attendant with the autumn-coloured hair is purple rather than red. Keep your pear ripe, my friend, for upon our return I swear you could dip it in that honey jar."

Ruadhán scowled at the young man's coarse comments and stalked from the room towards the courtyard. He was not impressed by the company his uncle Aedric kept.

With all the preparations finished, Ruadhán stood before the mounting block as a squire held his horse steady. He had made his farewells but, in truth, he was eager to be away. It was a time of mixed emotions. Excitement tinged with anxiety of what was to come. Since they were all mounted, they could move at speed and it would only take them a few days to ride to the coast, where the square-rigged and single-masted cogs would be gathering to transport them to Brest.

They landed in Brittany on the fourteenth of August.

"We shall make merry here, lads," someone shouted as they sat around their fires two days later. "Charles de Blois is already raising his siege, and word has it he'll withdraw and will likely form up forty miles east from here."

The devastating defeat of the English by the Scots at Bannockburn and the lessons learned at the battles of Dupplin Moor and Halidon Hill ten years before, would shape the fight to come. Since Ruadhán's own lord at Folkingham, Henry de Beaumont, took a leading hand in the design of the change in strategy, he was well-placed to understand how the forthcoming battle was likely to play out. Ruadhán's excitement at the chance to prove himself was high.

Men-at-arms and archers alike would dismount while squires and attendants would hold the horses behind the lines, in case there warranted a quick escape. No longer was a mounted charge deemed to be effective.

The evening before the battle, Ruadhán visited the scribe and asked him for some scraps from his bin. The man handed him a piece of parchment with a small hole where the scribe had scraped it too thin, but it would be good enough. He settled to write a quick missive to the Lady Emma. He knew she could not read, but trusted that Mistress Clémence would help. The messenger would speak in person to his uncle Aedric.

After considering what to say, he bent his head to the task. Once completed and sent, he considered he had undertaken his lordly duty.

My dear,

My courser has served me well, although I confess I miss the glamour of riding a destrier into battle. After a full day and more in the saddle, we have arrived at a town on the Rivière de Morlaix with an advantageous position. We are anticipating a good day on the morrow. The men are excited and full of anticipation for success and God willing we shall do well. Our cause is worthy and I have sent prayers that I may excel in the field.

I hope all is well on my manor and that Sir Aedric is tending to his duties there to ensure a good harvest.

I send my felicitations to you and your companion.

Ruadhán, Lord Amundeville du manoir, Grimsthorpe, Soke of Folkingham, Lincolnshire.

Lady Emma sat in her solar, gazing across the gloomy room as the rain pounded the window coverings. She had demanded candles, despite the expense, and Clémence was glad of the woven hangings on the walls that helped to keep the room warm. A fire blazed and servants were kept busy supplying logs to maintain the flames. It would soon be time to affix the shutters for winter. Clémence tried to distract her mistress from her despondency. Chess had been a short-lived diversion, with the young noblewoman sighing and making mistakes through lack of concentration.

Although Clémence disliked sewing, she had noted that Emma sometimes worked on small pieces of embroidery.

"Why don't we start a larger piece?" Clémence suggested. "Did you hear of a tapestry of enormous proportions undertaken in the eleventh century? My father told me of it. He has travelled in northern France and saw the work."

Emma shook her head but Clémence saw that she had her attention.

"The Conqueror King's half-brother, named Odo, commissioned it to embellish his new cathedral. The piece tells the story of kings, knights and peasants."

"What is the story?"

"It begins when Edward the Confessor —" Clémence crossed herself at the name of the sainted monarch — "instructed Harold Godwinson, his brother-in-law, to go across the sea to Normandy to invite his cousin, William, to accept the crown of England. But instead Harold decided to take the crown for himself, saying Edward had promised it to him."

"Had he?"

"It was complicated. Rumour has it that Edward promised it to several as a means of diplomacy and keeping everyone happy. Anyway, the tapestry depicted a terrible battle. The end of the story is missing, but the panels finish with Harold's troops fleeing from William's and Harold's own death — struck through the eye by an arrow!"

Emma sighed. "What story have we to tell? There is nothing so dramatic. And anyway, my loom is not satisfactory for such a sizeable task."

"It's called a tapestry but in fact it's an embroidered story. Our tapestry tale doesn't need to be as long as that one. It's nearly two hundred and fifty paces in length."

Emma's eyes widened. "Really?"

"We should embroider our story, too, not weave it. We could start with Sir Ruadhán and his men leaving for Brittany. We observed that together, so we would know what to include."

Emma was enthusiastic. "Let us find Goodwife Joan. She will have some linen for our groundwork and then you must sort our threads and see which colours will be of use."

Over the next few days, Clémence and Emma worked together on a design for the first panel. The charcoal outline was clear enough. Emma shied away from working on the central figure and was far more enthusiastic about fashioning the horses and the accompanying knights with their weapons.

"Ow!" exclaimed Clémence.

Emma smiled. "Pricked your finger again?"

"I wish there was something to cover the tip of this finger to protect it." Clémence sucked the drop of blood away.

One day as they worked companionably on yet another wet day, they heard the pounding of hooves.

Emma threw down her work and opened the shutter a crack to see what the commotion was. Clémence hurried to stand at her shoulder, straining to see. A stranger had arrived, looking tired and muddy. His horse was steaming despite the rain, and she guessed he had ridden hard. "I do believe it is a messenger," said Emma.

Clémence's heart began to thud. She feared unwelcome news from one arriving at such speed.

"What do you think it's about?" Emma asked.

"Perhaps we might descend and ask?" Clémence replied.

"I don't think Sir Aedric would brook interference from me," Emma said. "Although he did consult me with regard to whether I would like to engage some minstrels for our entertainment." She smiled at the memory.

Although this was news to Clémence, right now she was tense with frustration at not knowing the messenger's information.

"We might go to the head of the stairs and listen," Clémence suggested. "Then, when the messenger has delivered his story and gone to the kitchens, we could say we saw him arrive and ask what he did say."

"Yes, that's a good idea." Emma brushed a few remaining clippings of thread from her kirtle and then moved towards the door.

They were just in time to hear Aedric's deep tones.

"Yes, I am lord of this manor," he said.

Clémence frowned. *Oh no you are not, even if you are enjoying the wine cellar so much*, she thought to herself.

The messenger bowed low. "I come from Portsmouth, sir. One of the merchant's cogs was commissioned to take sealed letters for London and Sir Ruadhán told me to come too. My wife is near her term and he thought I —"

"Yes, yes, man!" Aedric waved his arm with impatience. "Get to the point."

Clémence was as frustrated as Aedric and could barely contained her own irritation at the man's procrastination.

"If my lord is wounded or worse, what will become of me?" whispered Emma.

Clémence put a finger to her lips as she strained to hear.

The messenger spoke. "We arrived at a place on the river near a town called Morlaix."

The young women looked at each other, praying that all had gone in Ruadhán's favour.

CHAPTER 9

It was mid-August before William de Bohun, first Earl of Northampton and his retinue arrived in Brittany after many frustrating delays. However, upon landing, it appeared that the Franco-Breton troops of Charles de Blois had fled, raising the siege of Brest without bothering to engage the much smaller English force. Forward scouts returned to Northampton's base to report that Charles had withdrawn to Guingamp, forty miles to the east.

Northampton and his forces followed, capturing Vannes on the way. Thus, it was nearly six weeks before the two forces were close enough to each other.

During the dark cloak of night there were muffled grunts and occasional curses as men dug the trench in front of their position. "This is bloody demanding work."

"You can say that again." Another leant on his spade to take a breath. "But if it stops the French getting to us, then it's worth it. It'll not be as deep as the one the Scots had at Bannockburn. That saved the Scots, so let's hope this one does the same for us."

When the two armies finally faced each other, it was following an unsuccessful siege of the small town of Morlaix by the English. On hearing that Charles de Blois was advancing with a huge force enlarged by the sympathetic French nobility of the region, the English left the town and formed up in front of a small wood.

"This is a reasonable position." Ruadhán spoke across the space between his horse and that of his friend, Stephen de Chesham.

"Aye, we have a slight advantage with the land sloping away from the road down there to the east," Stephen answered. He wiped his face with a cloth. It had turned mild and although still early morn, inside his own padding and armour, Ruadhán understood how his friend felt. "We want the bastards to advance towards us. We don't need to go down to them and up the other side of that valley towards Lanmeur."

"The woods will disguise our archers until they come forward on our flanks, and our horses will be hidden here among the trees until we have need of them." He spoke as he dismounted and prepared to line up, leaving the horses under cover, should they be needed for a hasty retreat.

Stephen crossed himself. "The strategy worked before, so let's hope the French haven't copied us and still favour a head-on charge."

"Amen to that and God be with us this day."

As the sun reached its zenith, they finally heard the clink of metal. In the distance, a cloud of dust announced the arrival of the enemy forces. All fell silent as the French army advanced slowly across the terrain. French infantry crossed the river and lined up on the flat land below, where the land began to rise towards the English, while their cavalry amassed behind, remaining on the far side of the river.

"God's teeth." Stephen swore inside his helmet.

Ruadhán's stomach clenched. The enemy forces were vast compared to their own. "How many do you reckon?"

Talk across the lines varied in their estimation. Some said as many as fifteen thousand.

"Christ's nails." Ruadhán surveyed the fluttering standards, the glint of sun on metal, the cloud of dust beginning to settle, revealing the troops of Charles de Blois. "There must be seven times as many of them," he said.

"Yes, but look! They're in three blocks. It's their traditional formation."

A familiar rush of adrenalin shot through Ruadhán at the expectation of what was to come.

The order came to move forwards and line up. The knights did as bid, leaving the horses with the attendants and squires. The archers moved on either side of them to take positions on their flanks. Each archer was carrying a longbow and arrows of two and a half feet in length. The bows had a draw weight of around one hundred pounds, and every man was confident his arrow would travel six hundred feet. They had all seen the devastation their flight could induce once the advance began.

"Here they come." The English watched as the first ranks of infantry began to walk forwards in formation, gradually increasing their speed until they were running across a mile of territory.

"They're nothing but a bunch of peasants with billhooks and staves," Ruadhán shouted in amazement.

A roar of laughter and cheers rang forth as the archers from the sides pulled their bow strings and let loose the first wave of death. Loading fresh arrows every five seconds, it took a mere second and a half to travel the three hundred feet that remained between them and their target. The enemy dropped to the ground among screams and moans and it wasn't long before those who were left standing fled the battleground.

A pause ensued before the English began taunting with shouts and jeers.

The second wave were mounted men-at-arms and knights, who took the charge, little expecting the trench the English had previously dug.

"Get ready archers! Aim for those who have crossed the trench." A further wave of arrows flew with a dull whistle, causing further chaos as men and horses fell. There were cries as men were pinned beneath horses and had bones shattered. The first ranks of dismounted English strode forward into the chaos, weapons at the ready for hand-to-hand fighting.

As Ruadhán engaged in the battle, all his training and experience took hold and became unthinking actions, making short work of his first opponent who had a sword and small metal buckler shield. He feinted a cut to the man's outside arm, causing him to separate his sword from his buckler, thus enabling Ruadhán to deceive with a thrust in between to the soldier's neck. The second was despatched as quickly with a few cuts to form a star — cutting across, rolling his hand before cutting backhand, then up and back again. His opponent, clearly less experienced, became mesmerized with Ruadhán's speed and dexterity. There was as much wrestling as skill with weapons. Ruadhán understood how to swing his opponent round to damage his shoulder, and how to fell him with a blow to the back of his knees and finish him off before he could arise. Although good armour could be heavy, most knights were adept at rising speedily enough, but Ruadhán was quick and no one could get the better of him. He worked with instinct as well as practice.

The metallic smell of blood was thick in the air. Sword thrust and slash, or the blunt force of a superior weapon, would all cause death if aimed at the right spot. When a man went down with dehydration, exhaustion, or heatstroke, he was easy prey for a sword point. The palms of the hands were particularly vulnerable. Joints in armour under armpits, behind knees, or a stab through a visor opening, dispatched many. *Where's Geoffrey de Charny? Where is the French knight?* Ruadhán looked around for Charny's standard. From the corner of his eye he caught someone rushing him. He turned, parried, slashed and thrust, aware of blood spurting over his visor from his opponent. He cast about for his next opponent before the man even hit the ground.

Stephen was fending off two men. Ruadhán rushed to his aid across ground wet with blood. He nearly slipped, but managed to right himself before charging his shoulder into one of the French soldiers. Momentarily off balance, it gave Ruadhán the opportunity to swing his mace and it came down upon the fellow's helmet with a resounding clang, leaving such a deep dent that the effect on the man's skull was beyond dispute.

Stephen and Ruadhán took a moment to view the retreat of the remaining force.

Some of the men-at-arms jeered and chased for a few steps, but the rout was decisive.

"Come, friend," Stephen said to Ruadhán, "our work here is finished for the time being and I am in need of water."

"Let's hope Charles decides against sending his third wave. Surely he has suffered enough humiliation." Ruadhán turned to follow his friend.

Upon regrouping, the men removed their helmets to quench their thirst, before turning so see the third French wave had paused again.

"I take it that is not your blood spattered across your face, my good man," said Stephen.

"No. 'Twas that last fellow. I caught a small gap between his helmet and gorget."

"God's teeth," Stephen swore. "It must have spurted with some force."

"Aye, it did." Ruadhán grew suddenly serious. "I do believe they will come again. Look!"

Sure enough, the third wave were lining up across the shallow valley.

Stephen nodded. "Our trench will be no surprise now."

"They still have more men than our whole army, and look how wide they are spread on our flanks. Our archers are in danger of being threatened from the side and they must be low on arrows by now."

"My Lord Northampton is calling us to moot. Perhaps he has a plan," Stephen said.

Clémence and Emma moved to the top step and began to descend. The messenger was now in full flow.

"Then my Lord Northampton produced a bold plan, and most unusual. I'm unsure if it was ever done before."

"Yes, man. Get on with it. This story is becoming overlong." Aedric, forever impatient, urged the messenger to get to the decisive point, but he swayed not from his account. He continued, as charged, to deliver the whole, in person.

"He withdrew his forces in good order and —"

"Withdrew?" Aedric cut in. "He gave up?"

"No, my lord, they withdrew into the woods."

Aedric frowned in puzzlement.

"It was indeed a magnificent stroke, sir. They formed a hedgehog line, each facing the outward direction. My Lord Northampton charged the archers to reserve their bows until the French were close enough to smell them and then to aim with care and pick them off one by one."

"Were the French mounted?"

"Yes, sir, in the old traditional way. You should have heard those arrows whirr. Each one found its mark, toppling the men from their horses. The animals either fled or caused more confusion, leaving the men to their fate."

"And?"

"And the French deserted on all sides, sir."

"Come," said Emma, "let us descend."

"Ah, my dear." Aedric caught sight of them and waved Emma forward. He smiled with charm at the young bride-to-be. "Come and join us, sweet girl." He indicated a chair next to him.

Clémence stood behind her and watched, with surprise, as Emma greeted Aedric and matched his smile with her own before casting her eyes down.

The messenger bowed his head to acknowledge their presence before continuing. "There were perhaps fifty French knights slain that day and three times that many taken hostage, including Geoffrey de Charny, no less. He'll fetch a lively ransom. Many more common men died in the field."

Clémence could stand it no longer. "And what of our army, sir? What of Lord Ruadhán?"

Aedric frowned at her before he too, asked, "And our losses?"

"Light, sire. Exceptionally light, and Sir Ruadhán was celebrating in good health."

Clémence let out the breath she hadn't realised she had been holding.

"Battle tactics have changed," the man continued, "but the French and Genoese have not realised it. And more, they still rely on the crossbow rather than our five-feet longbows. Far superior and proven."

"When might Sir Ruadhán return? Will it be soon?" Emma asked with a small glance at Aedric.

"Nay, my lady. They have gone on to lay siege to the town of Morlaix again, and other battles may follow. King Edward is determined to make secure his lands in Gascony. He will not forgive Philip of France for supporting the Scots against us and he maintains his right to the throne of France through his decent from the French princess, Isabella."

"The She-Wolf of France," Aedric said, disparagingly, but his next words shocked Clémence even more.

"Shall we ride out later today, my dear? The weather is improving." He turned to Emma, bestowing her with his most charming smile.

"Oh yes, sir, it would be such a pleasant change." Turning to Clémence, Emma said, "Perhaps you would like the day to visit your family. I shall be engaged with the outing and shall not need you."

"Oh, but will you not need accompanying?" Clémence dearly wished to go home and visit her mother, if only for a few hours, but she would not neglect her duty to Lady Emma.

"You heard my lady," Aedric said. "We shall be a merry company and do not require your services."

"Yes, sir." Clémence dropped her gaze.

"In fact, stay overnight and return in the morn. There are plenty here who may wait on our young lady."

"I shall return before nightfall, my lord," Clémence said. "There will no longer be a place for me to sleep at home." This was a fabrication, but she was determined not to leave Emma alone overnight.

"Oh yes, indeed. Return to me before nightfall," Emma said. "In the meantime, I shall enjoy a ride out with the other ladies and the few remaining menfolk." She cast her eyes around the company, who had gradually been arriving over the last day or two.

This is becoming increasingly Aedric's home, Clémence thought, and hoped that Ruadhán would return soon, before this grasping man succeeded to more that his lot. Was his plan to take on Lady Emma as well as the ordering of the household? There were dangers at home as well as in France, it seemed.

It was mid-morning when Clémence arrived home to rapturous joy from her family.

"Where is Father?" she asked, after extricating herself from their embraces.

"He is away to the abbey. The building works on the wool house extension are progressing well and when he is not working on that he spends hours at his bench, carving the statuary for the abbey."

"Yes, of course. Perhaps I might go and see how his work proceeds."

Catherine chuckled as she rocked the baby — who had been named Arthur. "My, you even talk like a noble-born lady, now." She turned to Agnes, who had resumed her spinning. "You might like to go with your sister."

"Thank you but no, Mother. I should like to do a little more of this before the Sext bell and we stop for our midday meal."

"I shall make speed, then, and be back in time for that, too." Clémence hurried out of the door and took the path to the abbey.

The morning was fresh, despite the sun. Clémence breathed deeply and relaxed as she heard the familiar calls of the birds and the wind rustling the leaves above her head. She smiled at the sight of the brown earth in the distant field, knowing another harvest must be stored safely despite the recent rains. She remembered the comforting presence of Father Robert. It was many months since he had departed for the Mother House in Yorkshire and she wondered how he was. She hoped not to meet Father Deodonatus, but perhaps he was out seeing to his ministrations in the wider community.

As she neared the solid grey stone walls of the abbey, there was comfort in knowing its permanence in their lives. She remembered seeing the monks swaying as they walked in two regular lines along the lane in their grey-white robes on a Sunday afternoon and chanted their prayers in their church. As young children, sometimes she and her siblings had been to watch them at work in the fields and on occasions received an invitation to help them with the haymaking.

Clémence turned the corner on the way to her father's workshop when she came to an abrupt halt. Coming towards her was Father Deodonatus. She could not avoid him.

"Mistress Clemence," he said. "I hope you are taking regard of your soul at the manor house. There are many temptations in such a place."

"Yes, indeed, Father." Clémence bobbed a curtsey.

"I have not seen your sister in church for a while. I visited your home, of course, to ensure your mother is secure in the love of God, but Mistress Agnes is not always there to receive my blessing."

Clémence glanced up and caught the flick of his tongue. "She is busy in the house and helping Mother with the baby, since Mother is unable to do much."

"Of course. Yes indeed. She is very devout and I enjoy our discussions very much when I do see her."

"Forgive me. I am going to see my father and view the progress of his new carvings for the refectory. I don't have long before I must return home and thence to return to my duties at the manor."

"Of course. God speed and may His blessings be on you. Remember to tell your sister to come to church for confession soon."

"Yes, Father." Clémence bobbed another curtsey and hurried on her way to the workshops.

Later, as Clémence walked back to the cottage, she had another encounter which was also not particularly welcome.

"Daniel! What brings you here at this hour? Are you well?"

"I heard you were home for a while. I went to see Agnes, but she was busy, so I thought to come and find you. I have waited long enough for your sister, but she seems determined to lead the life of chastity. So what about you, Clémmie? Will you marry me?"

Clémence's heart sank. She must be fair and honest with him now. This could not continue. "Daniel, it is not to be. Not now and not in the future. You must look elsewhere, for I …" She trailed off as she saw his expression darken. "I'm sorry, Daniel. Truly I am."

"Perhaps you might think again and look kindly upon me, Clémmie." Daniel's tone became wheedling. "We've known each other for many years. I would make a good husband."

"You would, Daniel." She spoke gently. "But not for me. I am working at the manor, as you know, and am happy there."

Daniel stared at her before he turned and left. He shouted back over his shoulder when several feet away. "Then I shall go and fight for someone who will appreciate my strength and loyalty. There are plenty of knights who will be pleased of my services."

Clémence was shaken by his anger, but also pleased that the matter had finally been settled.

CHAPTER 10

Life at the manor house continued with Clémence and Emma playing chess, walking outside when the weather was warm and dry, and they continued to sew their story. The new panel was a depiction of the men at battle as reports continued to arrive of the defeat of the French at Morlaix and the subsequent siege of the town which, in the end, did not go in favour of the English. Emma also spent time riding out with Aedric more frequently.

Clémence was increasingly concerned and ventured to mention it after a particularly long absence, when the accompanying men returned an hour or so before Aedric and Lady Emma. Now Emma tossed her head haughtily. "It's not for you to question what I do."

"I'm only concerned that folk will talk, my lady."

"You go too far, Clémence," Emma said, using her full name in anger. "Aedric is a kind man who is simply looking after me while Ruadhán is away. Nothing more."

"Yes, my lady. Forgive me."

"You may help me brush my skirt. It has become creased and dusty where I was sitting on it astride the saddle."

Clémence moved forwards, determined to say no more.

"Aedric has been showing me how to fly the new merlin he has given me. Of course, his saker falcon is well used, but my bird is inexperienced, as am I. He was exceedingly kind and showed me how to hold the tether by standing behind me and placing his hand on mine."

Clémence bit her lip. A chill slithered down her spine. She was becoming more certain that Aedric was attempting to steal

Ruadhán's birthright. She would wait but watch with care. Surely her lord must return soon. Emma was innocent indeed.

Conversation turned. "We saw your father at one point. Apparently, the new wool house is progressing well and Abbot Walter is using the wool grant to reduce the debt. It was three hundred and twenty-two pounds. Can you imagine? Such a vast sum. Hopefully the extension that your father is building will mean they are able to process more wool."

"It can only be good for the whole of Grimsthorpe," Clémence said. "They will take more sheep and not only will the abbey's debt be reduced, but perhaps the farmers may benefit, too."

It was only a few weeks later that lookouts stationed at the perimeter of the manor raised a warning that a mounted company were approaching. Clémence, unsure if it was celebration or trouble, hurried to see what might be happening. These were uncertain times, and Lady Emma had not yet returned from her latest excursion with Aedric.

As the company neared, Clémence was delighted to see a banner she recognised. Lord Ruadhán and his men-at-arms had returned with a flurry of activity and noise.

As the horses were led away to be fed and rested, the heavy coffers carried indoors, and the armour removed to the blacksmith to be mended and the weapons sharpened, the men demanded food and ale. Joan commanded all hands to cut, chop, peel and cook. She shouted at the spit boy for not rotating the spit with the meat on it fast enough, and Hawise scrubbed pots endlessly.

Rejoicing was great in the hall, and it wasn't long before the timbre of deep male voices, already in their cups, were laughing and sharing tales of daring and courage.

"Where is my bride-to-be?" Ruadhán demanded. "And my uncle, where is he?"

Clémence stepped forward anxiously, noting his smell of a hard ride in the saddle, his strong physique and flaming hair. "He is not yet returned from a ride, my lord. Sir Aedric has been teaching my Lady Emma to hunt with a merlin."

"I see." Ruadhán's expression clouded before he moved away to join the other men.

It wasn't long before Lady Emma and Sir Aedric returned. At the same time, Father Deodonatus appeared, silent as a wraith and looking suitably humble.

Aedric swaggered through with loud and effusive praise for the men's successes in battle, ignoring the ignominious laying of the siege at Morlaix. He slapped his nephew on the back, guffawing as he did so. Emma, meanwhile, shrank into the background, almost standing behind Clémence as she took off her cloak.

Father Deodonatus was obsequious in his praise. "Master, welcome home. God be praised that you are safe and in one piece." He made the sign of the cross over the company. "As your own priest is away, perhaps we might gather in the church for a thanksgiving before the night is through."

"Tomorrow, Father. Right now, we have ridden a long way and we need food and rest. Return tomorrow at Terce and we will say our thanks then. That will give us time to rise and we will worship before the start of the day."

Before they knew it Christmas was upon them and all thinking put to the preparation of the feast.

For the monks, freshly tonsured for the last part of advent as a sign of their devotion and humility, time was spent in song, contemplation, and prayer. For the rest of the community, from the fourth Sunday of Advent until Christmas eve, fasting helped to concentrate the mind upon the festivities to come, although they did not observe the abstinence to the same degree as the monks.

In the kitchens, Joan had prepared the pig, slaughtered the previous month, and now the black pudding, hams, and bacon were resting on the shelves and on the cold slab. Aedric had ordered trout and even lampreys. There were tarts, custards, nuts, and sweetmeats. For the poorer villagers, the kitchen prepared the umbles from the pig and also a deer, too inferior for the Christmas feast. They were mixed with apples, bread and blood, and seasoned well. The umble pies that emerged from the oven would be well-received by those who struggled throughout the rest of the year.

"We need to plan the entertainment," Emma said. "Who will be the Christmas Bishop?"

Clémence frowned in thought. "It must be someone who is well-deserving. To receive that honour of playing the role of the bishop, it must go to someone who has earned the place."

Their choice of clothing was a topic of much discussion and Clémence was enchanted with a cast-off dress that Lady Emma offered her. The fabric was the smoothest she had ever known and the colour enhanced the green in her eyes. It was perfect for the Christmas celebrations, and she added little bows of red ribbon to both the dress and a garland of leaves and berries Lady Emma had helped make for her hair.

When the day arrived, excitement filled the air and Clémence held her head up high.

All the unmarried younger people gathered in a circle. The young man selected to play the Christmas Bishop stood on a chair in the centre.

"Are we ready?" Emma asked.

"Yes, we are ready," came a chorus of voices.

All the maids, including Hawise and Marie, as well as the boys from the stables and the kitchens ran around him three times, calling, "We consecrate a Christmas Bishop *pro nobis*."

The playful ritual complete, the older men and women clapped and cheered, and quaffed yet more wine with liberty. By the time the 'Bishop' came to playfully 'marry' people for the night — as many couples as he wished, and for one night only — all would be merry enough to go along with it. In the meantime, he would retire to his corner and practise his strange faces and feigned voice.

It was late in the afternoon when the sound of singing floated through the frosty night air. Clémence clapped her hands and almost flew to the door. Ruadhán had ordered the gate left open in anticipation.

As Clémence watched, a raggle-taggle group of mummers approached. "Is that Mattie? There, on the end with that tall man who, I do declare, is my father," she cried with glee to Emma. "Look! My brother has on the boar's mask." Her heart leapt with pride to see her young brother joining in the festivities with the villagers. In the topsy-turvy atmosphere of the celebrations, some of the men were dressed as women, while some of the women were dressed as men and even had charcoal beards.

"Come in, enter this hall and bring us good cheer." Ruadhán laughed and opened the huge door wide so the company might caper around the hall, receiving gifts of coins and sweetmeats to fill their pockets.

By the time the mummers had left and the vast quantities of food and wine consumed, it was time for the Christmas Bishop to perform.

"I choose first," he said in a weird squeaky voice, and he paused for effect, "Hawise Webb, daughter of Paul the Weaver."

The young woman looked about her in fascinated terror.

"I marry her to John Bennett. Blessed in surname and blessed in nature. Come forward both."

Clémence watched as Hawise crept forwards. The women from the household were smiling. One or two of the men cheered. She didn't like the look on Aedric's face, and she said a silent prayer of thanks that it was not he who young James had called forward. The 'Bishop' repeated the process twice more and it looked as if that would be all.

Clémence looked around the company. Some were swaying, fully in their cups, others had collapsed against the wall. One or two were getting amorous. While Christmas celebrations at home had been effusive and unrestrained, she had not known so much celebratory excess before.

"I call Clémence Masson, daughter of Merek the Mason."

What? Surely he did not mean to call her name. Clémence looked around, confused. Someone nudged her arm.

"Go on, Clémmie." Joan was standing next to her. "It's only a bit of fun."

Clémence heard her name again and there was rhythmic clapping. She moved through the crowd to stand before the Christmas Bishop.

"I marry her to…" The pause seemed endless. *Please Lord let it not be Sir Aedric*, thought Clémence.

"… Sir Ruadhán."

Clémence glanced across at Emma, who was standing next to Sir Aedric. She was laughing and showed no sign of displeasure.

Sir Ruadhán approached. "Perhaps we might stroll outside for a while?" he said. "Go and fetch your shawl — the night air is chill."

Clémence looked up at him. She knew this man well after all these months, but she was unsure what he expected of her and a prickle of apprehension ran down her spine.

Her anxiety must have shown on her face, for Ruadhán gave a gentle laugh. "Don't be frightened. All we will do is walk, and talk for a while, to satisfy the company."

Clémence wasn't sure if she was relieved or disappointed, but as she ran to fetch her shawl, she was grateful that her maidenhead was not in jeopardy. She did not wish to lose her position here at the manor, nor a lecture from Father Deodonatus for tempting Sir Ruadhán into sin.

When she descended, she slipped outside to meet Ruadhán on the front steps. He took her elbow and guided her through the dark towards the gardens, which were silent in the frosty air. The square beds smelled of rosemary, thyme and sage, and winter savory brushed her skirt as she moved past, emitting its own aromatic scent. The pathways were wide enough for them to walk side by side. The bench at the far side fashioned from woven willow beckoned, and Ruadhán guided Clémmie towards it.

"Tell me," he said, "are you happy here?"

"Indeed, I am, sir."

"Please, call me by my given name. Ruadhán — the red one." He laughed. "No person can be in doubt about why my name was chosen. My mother was fanciful and remembered her grandfather across the sea in Ireland." He passed his hand over his bearded chin.

Clémence smiled and began to relax. "My Lady Emma is generally very kind and we have become friends," she said.

"Generally?" Ruadhán said, raising an eyebrow. "You mean she always gets her way and she is spoiled by it. It is Clémence, is it not?"

"Yes, from the Latin *clemens*, meaning mercy and mildness. But my family call me Clémmie."

Ruadhán looked at her. "Tell me, from where did you achieve so much learning. It is unusual in one of your position and sex."

"My father allowed me to learn with Father Robert at the abbey. He was very well-travelled before he came here. There are so many places of interest that I should love to visit — the great cathedrals of France, the art in Italy. Giotto di Bondone, who recently died," she crossed herself, "produced some wonderful works."

Ruadhán threw back his head and laughed uproariously. Clémence was thankful they sat far removed from the house and the company within, who were becoming loud and boisterous themselves, and would not hear.

"You are more of a surprise each day," Ruadhán said. "Indeed, it pleases me greatly."

Clémence shivered, unsure if it was the chill of the night or at his words.

"Come, let us wander back. You are cold."

Arriving near the steps, Ruadhán stopped walking and turned to Clémence. "I am loathe to re-enter the hall. I have no wish for more wine. I've enjoyed our talk."

"As have I … Ruadhán."

He placed one finger below her chin and raised her face gently. "Thank you, Clémmie. I may have to leave for battle in France again soon, but I shall take the memory of this night with me. He lowered his face but stopped before his mouth met hers. His breath on her face was sweet with wine and anticipation engulfed her.

She leaned imperceptibly closer and their lips touched. His lips were warm and dry, his beard soft against her chin. Her lips parted against his and his hand move around to the back of her head as the kiss intensified.

Suddenly, Ruadhán pulled away. "You enter the hall first," he said. "I have things to do. I need to visit the stables."

Her breath ragged, Clémence mounted the first step and when she turned, Ruadhán was already taking long strides away.

Clémence slipped up to Lady Emma's chamber and was happy to wait there for her mistress to return. As she waited, she opened her box of treasures. She fingered the intricate carving that Ruadhán had slipped into her hand all those months ago, the carved comb her father had made, and the most recent piece of embroidered tapestry tale upon which she was working. Then she placed one of the red ruffles from her dress inside the copper-lidded box.

As she lay on her mattress, she smiled to herself as Ruadhán's words echoed in her memory. Whether it was this or the wine, but it wasn't long before she drifted into a deep sleep. When she awoke it was still dark, but she heard the bells chime for Prime in the distant abbey. It was time to rise.

Her first thoughts were of puzzlement. Surely Emma would have woken her when she had returned and needed help to undress for bed. Perhaps she had managed the laces herself?

Clémence fumbled quietly and found the fire steel, tinder box with its char cloth, and splint with which to light a candle. With practised ease the smell of beeswax soon filled her nostrils. None of the cheap tallow candles for Lady Emma.

When she held the light aloft, she saw that Emma's bed was empty.

Her mistress would certainly not have risen early, especially after the Christmas celebrations, which could often last until the early hours. So where was she?

As Clémence was trying to contain her panic, the door opened and Emma's face peered around.

"My lady! Emma! I have been worried for your safety."

"Really, Clémmie, what harm could come to me here? I have Aedric to watch out for me. I must be permitted some fun after all these months of waiting and stitching." She sounded like the old peevish Emma. "I shall to bed for a few hours now. You may help me. I've had a most enjoyable time. Aedric looks after me so well."

With apprehension in her heart, Clémence undertook her tasks.

The celebrations continued until twelfth night, and both young women had fun. Manorial business resumed as usual following the new year festivities, followed shortly after by halimote in January, when those who served on the land and in the mills and forges, came to the manor to pay their dues and settle grievances.

There was no indication from Ruadhán of the kiss they had shared on that beautiful crisp evening at Christmas. Clémence could not help but watch as he moved around the manor and courtyard, always ensuring to looking away and appear busy when he came close.

One morning, as she waited for Lady Emma to rise, Clémence took the opportunity to listen from the stairs to the halimote taking place in the great hall. It was the first time she had witnessed the proceedings and her insatiable curiosity got the better of her.

John, son of John Abovebrook, came into court for a debt of thirty-two pence which he had failed to pay from the year before. His fine was a further hefty forty pence, and he was told to be obedient henceforth. The seneschal collected the fine as the Lords Amundeville watched from the side.

Clémence could see from her hidden vantage point that the clerk was writing on his long and narrow parchment. There were several errors in syntax and he employed many abbreviations. She was of a mind that she could do better.

It seemed the court was lenient towards the destitute and realistic about being able to raise money where there was none. On occasion, Sir Ruadhán would interrupt and say, "In mercy, you are fined, but pay nothing this time. Your name is in the ledger, however, so do not re-offend. Unlike our Lord God — " he made the sign of the cross — "my patience is not infinite."

Clémence watched as Aedric raised his eyes to the rafters and, even from her position, heard the click of his tongue. He obviously cared little for Ruadhán's display of empathy.

Robert of Edenham's fine of one half penny was for carrying away the fittings of a plough belonging to William Wood. Simon Reeve accused Gilbert Farmer of malingering and working in his own barn and yard instead of performing his labour services, and so it went on.

The seneschal collected the fines and redistributed to those maligned. All were satisfied since all were under the same rules, and if the lord benefitted throughout, then such was life and Sir Ruadhán was fair-minded.

"Where are you? I wish to break my fast."

Clémence hurried through to the chamber, where Emma was sitting up in the bed, surrounded by down-filled pillows and cushions. "I want some wheat bread, it's softer than rye or oats. A little goat's milk perhaps?" she asked.

"Very well. I shall return with haste." Clémence hurried down the stairs to the hall and wove her way between the throng of workers, greeting those she knew well and nodding and smiling at others. She glanced across at Ruadhán and Aedric, who sat in their wooden chairs. Aedric held a posy of dried lavender and sage against his nose, and Clémence had to admit that the smell of the massed people was pungent. She was certain that Ruadhán was watching her as she made her way to the kitchens.

She had hardly seen him since Christmas. He had been away riding to collect the January dues, or hunting, and she had been entertaining Emma, when her lady was not out accompanying the men with her merlin as they were set their saker falcons to the air. On those occasions, she had taken the opportunity to mend clothes or sew a new day gown for herself from some fabric Joan had given her. This new one was in addition to the gown Emma had given her for the handfasting, and she was excited to finish it. The pale green colour suited her well and she had trimmed the hem with contrasting wool stitching in a similar pattern she had seen on one of Emma's dresses.

CHAPTER 11

Only a few months passed before skirmishes in France once more turned into battles. Word spread and even the lowliest of the servants at the manor knew that King Edward still claimed the crown of France, and that it was imperative that Philip VI was halted from entering Edward's lands in Aquitaine. Lord Stafford's campaign of siege and seize was not working, and the king dispatched Lord Derby to be more aggressive, a strategy that finally paid off when the French retreated from Bergerac. When the English laid siege to the regional town of Périgueux, Philip sent huge re-enforcements to the area, but the subsequent battle for the castle at Auberoche took the French by surprise. The English, angered by the capture of one of their messengers — who was subsequently hurled back at them from a siege catapult — once again successfully discharged their arrows.

The English-Gascon army's victory against a larger French force showcased their tactical prowess and resulted in considerable financial gain from ransoms of captured French noblemen. And three times the amount was made at Auberoche, further encouraging Edward III in his quest for the French throne.

At the manor, both Emma and Ruadhán seemed content with their current position and nothing advanced between them. Aedric continued in his role of kindly uncle to Lady Emma, although Clémence wondered if there was more between them. Perhaps not, as Emma remained with neither a ring nor a child. Perhaps Aedric was simply waiting to usurp

Ruadhán, knowing his nephew would be absent again before many more months.

Preparations for battle were ongoing. The noise of the forge continued day and night. Men were sent to harvest poplar and ash, both being sturdy enough for arrows, and the wood was piled high in a corner of the barn. The fletcher prepared his feathers, overseeing his apprentice to ensure each arrow had its flight from a single wing only, as he taught the boy each feather has one rougher side which made it spin. Clémence soaked up all this information as she walked between the manor house and the barns to help collect eggs or fetch the milk for the kitchens. Everyone was at full-stretch to ensure all was ready.

Finally, Lord Ruadhán and his men-at-arms were once more called to action in France. Sixteen thousand men landed on the coast of Normandy in July 1346. Welsh and English archers numbered seven thousand, for King Philip had still failed to recognise the effectiveness and strategic position ong of the English longbow. Not only were these forces critical, but the English Army also fielded five cannon that were smaller and lighter, allowing them to be moved around the battlefield more easily. The cannons fired stone ball projectiles, which were capable of causing much damage.

"Capturing Caen is an advantage," said Stephen de Chesham, Ruadhán's compatriot, as they arrived at the River Seine. "At least our backs should be safe."

"It's not going to be easy to find a crossing point. This is a mighty river and they have destroyed so many bridges."

They marched and rode along the bank of the river for several days before they found a bridge that they could mend sufficiently. They pillaged as they went to ensure they had enough food, leaving none for a following army.

"I was getting worried," Ruadhán said as they set a makeshift camp for the night. "Word has it that Philippe is assembling a mighty army in Paris and we were getting very close."

The next impassable barrier was the River Somme. It was hopeless, with all bridges destroyed, and land on either side becoming marshier as they marched back towards the coast.

"God's teeth, that was tough," Stephen said that night. "Praise the Lord the tide was out and we could just about manage the crossing."

Exhausted and soaked from wading through the river, they encamped in some woodland named Forêt de Crécy on the north bank of the Somme.

Ruadhán pointed. "Those clouds don't look too good."

"Forget the clouds, our scouts say they have an army six or seven times as large as ours," said Stephen.

"Our armour should keep us safe from their crossbows, but it's a good tactic to dismount as we have before and leave the horses behind. They're vulnerable and I wouldn't want to be trapped beneath mine."

"No," said Stephen. "You'd be a dead man then, my friend. Either crushed or at the end of a spear in no time."

Ruadhán was no coward, but the size of the opposition was fearsome, and he breathe deeply.

The French advanced as the sun passed its zenith.

"The twenty-sixth of August will be remembered," Ruadhán shouted above the clash of metal.

"For one reason or another," his friend shouted back.

The rain came in a sudden squall as Ruadhán heard the call. "Remove your strings. Stow them in your jerkins and hats." He watched the line of bowmen ahead and to the sides do as bid.

"Ha! The French cannot do likewise with their crossbows," someone shouted, and a cheer around him rose up.

"What are they doing?"

"The ground's so muddy they can't press the stirrups of their weapons and load."

"Where are all their protective pavises?"

"Must be in their baggage still."

As the French loaded their bolts and let loose with their bows, the wet strings would not pull sufficient weight and the arrows came to nought. Another jeer arose from the English, who hastily loaded their longbows and the arrows rained down. The five cannons added to the destruction.

"The enemy are running!" A cheer erupted from the English troops.

"Christ's blood, look down there, at the bottom of the slope. They can't get through the dead and the mud."

"The horses thrashing aren't helping. At this rate, our swords will be redundant."

Many French soldiers were crushed by falling horses or suffocated in the mud, and when the English and Welsh men-at-arms with spears and the knights with their swords attacked in close combat, the carnage was complete.

Clémence and Emma were in the manor gardens. Emma wanted to pick some sweet-smelling herbs for her chamber. The summer heat made the room stuffy. "I think I'll pick extra and present them to Aedric. His room needs them, even more than mine since it gets no shade." She flicked a glance at Clémence before adding, "I'll warrant."

With a shiver of unease, Clémence wondered how she knew this and was about to ask when they heard the thundering of hooves. They looked at each other, fearing bad news from

France. They had already heard that the French forces far exceeded their own in number.

"If Ruadhán is wounded, I shall not be able to nurse his wounds," Emma said. "There is simply no way I could countenance such a sight."

"Calm yourself, my lady," replied Clémence. "It is probably just a messenger to say battle is done, and you know our men have had immense success these last months."

They entered the hall to hear the latest news. "The battle raged on into the middle of the night, my lord," the messenger informed Sir Aedric. "It is said that following a long march King Philip wanted to wait a day, when his men would be rested, before attacking the English, but his nobles insisted on an immediate charge."

"And...?" Sir Aedric sat forward, eager to hear.

"Their arrogance resulted in the French defeat. King Philip finally left the field of battle and his men followed. The Welsh and Irish spears finished off the wounded."

"What of the king's son, Prince Edward? He is still young, but so brave and handsome, I hear," Emma said.

"The Duke of Alençon led a division of mounted knights and men-at-arms, including the blind King John of Bohemia, to attack his position. King John's horse was chained to those of his accompanying knights, but he fell in the field, as did they. I'm told the prince retrieved King John's standard and has adopted the motto *Ich Dien* — I Serve — as his own, as a mark of respect. The young prince served well, and King Edward has knighted the boy. He takes black armour and uses the colour now for his device."

"And what of our lord, Sir Ruadhán?" Clémence enquired.

"Oh yes, indeed," Emma added. "I too desire to know, of course."

"He is well, my lady. None of our knights were slain and only two taken prisoner for ransom. Of the troops only a handful died, unlike the French, who lost around three thousand. The battle has been an unprecedented military humiliation for the French. Our troops have now ridden with haste to lay siege to Calais, on the coast. If we can hold the town, it will be of major strategic import."

"Take this fellow to the kitchen, Clémmie, and see he is well fed," Emma said.

Clémence bobbed a curtsey and as she led the messenger away, she heard Aedric say, "Let us drink a toast to our success."

Our success, Clémence thought. *Huh! Little has he had to do with the success.* She was annoyed by his words. His life had not been in danger.

"Forgive me," said the messenger, interrupting her thoughts, "but are you Mistress Clémence?"

Upon her acknowledgement he continued in haste. "I have a message for you."

"From whom?"

"From Sir Ruadhán Amundeville." He held out a small piece of rolled parchment.

Footsteps sounded in the passage and Clémence grabbed the parchment from the messenger. "Come, sir, this way and someone in the kitchens will find food and ale for you. You have ridden far."

Clémence longed to open the missive, but she was never alone as she went about her tasks. Finally, as evening settled, Emma decided to stay by the fire and commanded Clémence to go to the chamber and prepare the bed for the night. Clémence curtseyed to the company and mounted the stairs at the far end of the hall. Once inside the chamber, she finally withdrew the small roll of parchment and read it eagerly.

My dearest Clémence,

We fare well and I am unscathed. The great meeting between us and the French last August has become known as the Battle of Crécy. It was won with ease. Their knights preferred death to the ignominy of retreat, according to the chivalric code, although several still fled dishonourably.

Now we are winning a siege against Calais on the coast, thanks to the result of that great battle, the ineptitude of King Philip, and his misunderstanding of our purpose. It will be a prominent place to hold for our troops to enter the north of France. Our great King's son, Edward, has become known as the Black Prince, due to the colour of his armour, and he is earning a name for himself in the field. We have recently built a fortification on the seaward side of the town and effectively have control of all that arrives. The Earl of Warwick covers the sea with eighty ships and all is but won here. I tell you this since I know you have a thirst for knowledge and would wish to know.

Enough! The reason I write is my concern for you. I hope to return once we have won this siege. I have missed your good sense and in truth I think of you increasingly.

There is a rumour that our people on the trade routes to the east are suffering a great plague, but so far there is no sign of it in France. I am sure we are secure and, as an island, England will not succumb.

Stay safe, my dear Clémmie.

I am your...

Here the ink had smudged. The journey the parchment had travelled was long and arduous, so it was not surprising.

Ruadhán Amundeville

Clémence ran her fingertips over his name, before hurriedly re-reading the missive. Surely, there was no mistaking the words. Hearing footsteps on the stairs, she rolled up the precious parchment and popped it inside her bodice. Later, she would place it with care in her box of treasures.

When Emma entered the chamber, she said, "I just found that little kitchen maid snivelling in a corner."

"Do you mean Hawise, who does the pots?"

"Probably. She scuttled off before I could ask her what was wrong." Emma continued before Clémence could ask more. "I'm going on a journey in a few months." She twirled around the room full of smiles and laughter.

"Oh?" This was news to Clémence.

"Yes, after the Christmas celebrations, and as soon as the weather allows and the roads are passable. It has become dull here. Only the angels know when Sir Ruadhán will return and anyway, I'm not sure I wish to be married to someone who is never here."

"It is written," Clémence said.

"Perhaps it should be unwritten, then," Emma snapped.

"Where might we go? To see your parents?" Clémence was curious. She was unsure she wanted to be elsewhere, especially since Ruadhán had said he would return after the siege of Calais was complete.

"Aedric has invited me to visit his manor. I shan't need you to come, though."

Clémence was shocked. "But my lady —"

"Undo my lacings, will you?" Emma turned to her companion so she might complete the command.

Clémence had a hollow in her stomach.

"You may stay here. I shall need you upon my return, for return I must, eventually," Emma said blithely. "There are maids aplenty at Aedric's manor and there will be company on the journey. I shall be very well."

"Sir Ruadhán may return soon, my lady." Clémence could not be more precise without revealing the message she had received from him.

"I'm tired of waiting. It could be months. He will have to wait upon *my* return should he finally decide to come home."

CHAPTER 12

Christmas with so many of the men away was a rather sober affair. There was just as much food, and plenty of ale and wine for those who wanted, but the atmosphere at the manor was lacking. There was no 'Christmas Bishop' appointed. Perhaps that was a good thing, as Clémence had no desire for him to pair her with anyone.

All her waking thoughts were of Ruadhán. There was no more news and the piece of parchment was becoming cracked with her constant handling of it when she was alone.

The weather had been cold and wet for weeks. Heavy grey clouds hung in the sky like a shroud. Clémence was running out of ideas with which to entertain an increasingly bored and petulant Emma. Their embroidery was increasing in size, with each panel illustrating their life at the manor, but it lacked inspiration during these winter months. It wasn't until February that clear skies and frost replaced the rain. Then the ground was as hard as metal and the ice on the bucket took an age to chip away. The time to leave for Aedric's home was imminent. He had sent a messenger to his manor a week before with word to prepare for a lady.

Clémence couldn't understand why Emma was taking such a rash decision to be with the uncle of her affianced.

"He is so kind and considerate," Emma said as she sat on the bed and watched as Clémence packed her boxes of clothes. "I do believe he loves me for who I am and not the marriage chest I would bring to my nuptials. He is most gentle with me."

Clémence was shocked. Did she mean they had already lain together? It would explain the long absences, when her own presence was not welcome. She was unsure how to ask the pertinent question and whether to warn against such dangerous behaviour. Everyone knew that it was a sin and especially outside of marriage. Aedric, at his age, should know better, though Emma would receive the blame for enticement, as all women did. Clémence was genuinely fearful for both Emma's soul and her safety.

"Emma, may I speak openly, as your friend?" she asked.

"Of course, Clémmie. You are my friend and confidante."

Clémence took a deep breath. "Sir Aedric minds your virgin status, does he not? As you are promised to his nephew?"

Emma looked down at her kirtle and plucked at the fabric. Then she raised her chin and spoke with authority. "It is not for you to question me in such a way. It is for you to finish packing my gowns. I'm going down to the hall. You will stay here and finish the task." With that she swept from the room.

Clémence had a sense of foreboding, but did as she was bid.

She hadn't seen the little maid, Hawise, for a day or two, when she saw the young woman in the courtyard the following morning. She looked tearful.

"Hawise, my dear, whatever is the matter?"

"Nothing, my lady. I was sick, that's all."

Clémence took a step back. Everyone feared illness.

"It's nothing. Something I ate, I'm sure."

"Have you asked Joan for an infusion of wormwood and mint? It may help."

"No, my lady. I'll be well enough later. It seems to come in the morn so I'll be right as rain by the time we hear the Sext bells."

"Go in now. You'll freeze out here," Clémence urged, before hurrying on her way. Having seen her mother become sick before birthing, she was worried for Hawise. The young woman had not the sense to repel a persuasive man. Thoughts of Father Deodonatus sprang to mind and his preachment on the sins of Eve. Hawise would not ask for assistance if she suspected she may be with child, although it was more likely she had no idea.

On the morning of the departure, as Clémence closed the lid of the last travel chest, she heard the sound of raised voices. She went to the open doorway and listened.

"I can't do everything in the kitchens without her," said Joan from below. "Gormless she may be, but she works hard enough and Marie won't do pots. And another thing, she shouldn't be able to walk off like that without a word to anyone. Sir, I think you should talk with her parents."

Aedric's deep tones followed. "Enough, woman! Don't be telling me my business. Hire someone else. That's your department. I have a journey to undertake."

Clémence frowned. She feared for both Hawise and Lady Emma. Oh, how she hoped Sir Ruadhán would return soon.

The courtyard was busy as the servants hastened to run messages, collect items, and back the horses up into the traces of wagons. Breath steamed from the animals' nostrils in the cold, bright morning. Clémence was not a part of the bustling activity. Instead she observed from the solar widow, having cracked the wooden shutter to air the room. She had said her farewell to Lady Emma in the great hall, the young woman awaiting her departure in a chair by the fire. Sir Aedric sat opposite her and she was laughing at some private remark he had made. Her excitement was palpable.

I wish Sir Ruadhán would arrive before they leave, Clémence thought for the umpteenth time. *Surely he would stop this madness.*

Clémence looked towards St Michael's church in the distance, but could see no sign of a column approaching. With a sigh she turned and sat down on the edge of the bed. She thought how easy it was for the two lords to come or go whenever they saw fit, and to stay away as long as they wished.

In the next moment she realised that it was, in truth, no easier for Ruadhán. He was at the request, no, demand of his overlord or monarch and faced danger every day. She retrieved the precious parchment he had sent her from her copper-lidded box of treasures. She had long since memorised every word, but still she looked at it. *I think of you increasingly.* She touched the words his hand had penned and then raised her fingers to her lips.

Before long, Clémence heard her mistress's high-pitched tones outside and she rushed to the window to peer down. As she watched, Aedric caressed Emma's cheek. She sighed. Nothing good could come of this.

A few minutes later, the cavalcade crossed the moat and shortly disappeared out of sight, heading north. They would not meet Ruadhán, should he return, since his path would be from the south coast.

Clémence took the opportunity to visit her home a few days later. After all, Emma had suggested she do so, and with the nobles away, Joan had given her consent. She packed a small bag and a few simple items of food to take with her for the day. She donned her warmest shawl, pulled her hood close, and braved the winter breeze and the icy paths to arrive at her parents' home later that morning. The greetings from her mother and Agnes were fulsome. She admired baby Arthur, who was sleeping in his box bed.

"Where are Father and Mattie? It's so cold to be working outside."

"They are both at the abbey. The outside walls of the wool house extension are complete and much of the inside. Carpenters have finished scaffolding around the pulpit and soon they will fit the new sculptures. Mattie is becoming skilled with wood and he helps with simple tasks. He finds it easier than stone."

"Are Father's sculptures finished?"

They discussed these for a few minutes before Clémence explained why she was able to leave the manor.

Catherine crossed herself and said, "A young lady, affianced to another and cavorting around the country. It is truly shocking behaviour."

Agnes similarly made the sign of the cross. "Perhaps you and I might go to church together and pray for her soul, Clémmie?"

Clémence's thoughts were more for Lady Emma's bodily safety rather than her soul, but she understood her sister's sentiment.

With fingers numbed by the chill air, Clémence and Agnes pushed open the huge wooden door of the church and entered the building. All was silent as the sisters moved to kneel in the nave. Having said their prayers silently, they moved to a stone bench against the wall where they might whisper together of more temporal matters.

After asking after the health of her mother and baby Arthur, Clémence asked, "And what of you, Sister? Do you visit here regularly?"

"I do not. Today, I know it is safe, but I don't wish to come on my own."

Clémence frowned. "Safe? What do you mean?"

"I don't want to meet … anyone."

"The only person you might meet is Father Deodonatus."

"Indeed," Agnes said.

"You do not wish to see Father Deodonatus? Where is he today?"

"He will be at the abbey. Saving his own soul, I hope," she added obscurely. "I have to see him when he visits Mother, but he unnerves me." She paused. "What I should really love to do is to retire from this world, so riddled with strife and sin, as it is. I should like to devote myself to God and contemplate how best to serve him."

"You do serve him, Sister. You are the most devout person I know."

"I mean exclusively, away from everyone."

"It will not be possible for you to join a nunnery, dearest. We have spoken of this with Father."

Agnes took a deep breath. "There will be a way. I must ask Father's advice."

Clémence shivered. "Let us return home. It is cold and Mother will be awaiting our return, hopefully with some warmed ale and a good pottage. I hope the vegetables and grain I brought have helped."

Dusk was falling when Clémence arrived back at the manor. Alone in the solar, she shed her shawl before finding a bowl of water in the kitchens to rinse the dust from her face and hands. She was pleased to discover that Hawise had returned to the manor. There was no time to speak with her, however, as Joan had her busy scrubbing pots again.

With little to do following Lady Emma's departure, Clémence scouted for an activity. She had a plan to occupy her mind and had consulted her father the last time she had seen him. In the absence of both lords, and under her decisive instruction, two men from the manor constructed a wooden water trough lined with clay to divert a small stream from inside the manor grounds. It ran across the moat rather than into it, and carried the water — and the bodily effluent of those who used it — some distance from the back of the house, into the woods. Now all foul water went far from the manor into the woods on the other side of the moat. Clémence was pleased with her idea. All that remained was to encourage all of the people to follow her example of carrying soil buckets away from the house. Surely they would see the benefits to health with greater cleanliness.

The following month, Clémence was sitting on the edge of the bed when she heard a commotion outside. She dropped her sewing and rushed to the head of the stairs. There was no mistaking the sound of clanking of metal and the stamp of horses' hooves. Perhaps Emma and Sir Aedric had returned and all could be forgotten before Ruadhán returned.

She hurried down the stairs, ready to wait upon her lady, before abruptly stopping.

Ruadhán strode across the rush-covered floor of the great hall towards her. His red hair was longer now, and his beard, too, which glowed in the sun behind him. Clémence longed to rush to him and into his arms, but the rest of the household had now gathered to welcome their lord home, and she held herself back.

"It's good to be home and among you all again. Food! My men must have food and ale!" Ruadhán shouted.

Typical that he should think of his men before himself, Clémence thought, as she hurried to the kitchen to ensure that Joan was aware of his return. Of course, she need not have worried for it was the housekeeper's task to know what was happening. She hesitated and looked around at everyone else who had a specific task as they bustled about their familiar surroundings. She was isolated, unable to serve him, unable to provide, unable to be close to him.

Several hours later the returning men had all been fed, the horses stabled, and the equipment sorted and sent for cleaning and repairing. Clémence had returned to the solar where she tried unsuccessfully to continue with her own sewing. She decided to go in search of something to wet her thirst before retiring for the night. Everything was quiet in the courtyard, and the servants were bedding down on their pallets at the end of the great hall. On silent feet she stepped over the rushes towards the kitchens, when Ruadhán's voice halted her progress.

"So, where is my bride-to-be? With my uncle it would seem, though no one is anxious to tell me all. Perhaps you will have the courage to enlighten me, Clémmie."

"Sir, I was instructed to remain here," Clémence said.

"When did they depart?"

"Lady Emma said she was wearied here and wanted some diversion." She tried to estimate how long they had been gone.

"I see. Could she not see that I was serving our king and not gone away of my own choosing?"

"I know not, sir."

"Sir?" He leaned towards her and spoke softly. "Am I not Ruadhán to you anymore? Sit, please. Keep me company, for I am tired and sore of heart. I have missed my home." He paused and, leaning over, he took her hand. "I have missed you."

Clémence was acutely aware that she must tread with care. "We have all missed you and I, in particular. But our positions are very different and you are affianced."

"It would seem that our handfasting means little to Lady Emma. How is she with my uncle?"

"I am genuinely uncertain. He is mild with her." Clémence recalled Aedric caressing Emma's cheek. The young noblewoman seemed enamoured of him.

"Mild, but not benign, I think. Long has he been working to usurp my place here. He is jealous of my position and thinks that he should be lord of this manor. Please, speak openly with me. No one else will, it seems."

Clémence took a deep breath. "You are correct. He flatters her with his attentions. I tried to persuade Lady Emma to take me with her, for I feared what may happen to her." She lowered her voice. "It may already be too late. Will you go to her now and bring her home?"

"Perhaps, but I shall think on it for a few days. I have no heart for it." Ruadhán dropped her hand and sat back in his chair. "There is another worry. In France we heard of a terrible pestilence sweeping west and north. It has come from the middle east. Apparently twelve ships from the Black Sea arrived in Messina in Italy this year and when people gathered on the docks a most horrifying sight met them. More sailors were dead than alive, and those who had not gone to God were gravely ill with black boils that oozed blood and pus."

Clémence gasped. "There are frequently seasonal plagues. Is this not normal? Although what you describe, I have never seen or heard of before."

"Sicilian authorities ordered the ships out of their harbour and we heard that they had landed again on the south coast of

France. There is a great mortality spreading throughout Europe." He shook his head in consternation.

"England is an island. Surely the sea will spare us — it is a natural barrier to such things," Clémence said.

Ruadhán nodded thoughtfully. "Perhaps you are right. I am weary, that's all."

"Perhaps it is time you retired to your chamber, things may appear less bleak in the morning."

Ruadhán heaved himself wearily from his chair and Clémence rose beside him, all thoughts of refreshments dissolving. At the top of the steps and out of sight of those settling in the hall below, he stopped and turned to her. "Thank you for your optimism. It is what I need right now." He placed his hands on her shoulders, with gentleness that the battlefield would not have recognised. He leaned in to place a kiss on her forehead, his beard soft as a feather and his lips warm.

As he stood straight and dropped his hands, Clémence smiled. "Sleep well, my lord." She watched him turn towards his own quarters. *May the angels guard us both*, she thought.

CHAPTER 13

Two days passed and still Ruadhán had not departed to fetch Lady Emma. For Clémence they were days of peaceful tranquillity. She went about her tasks and even began a new panel for the tapestry, which depicted Ruadhán's return. She wondered if she dared add her own portrait to the embroidery, but without Emma's presence, she was unsure what message it would portray. When she passed him in the great hall or a corridor, they exchanged a secret smile, and warmth spread through her body. The sight of him, his scent, his voice, commanding yet gentle, awoke a desire she had not experienced before.

On the third day there was a flurry of excitement outside the manor house. A travelling merchant had arrived. His two-wheeled cart, pulled by an ox, was large enough to carry a variety of goods, and he also had a string of donkeys with wicker paniers to help him transport his wares. It was an opportunity to buy new ribbons, tin mugs, carved ornaments, pots of all shapes and sizes, and even spices and perfumes. It was also an opportunity to hear what was happening elsewhere in the country.

Clémence rushed out across the moat with the others, eager to see what he had brought. The weather was set fair and the sun was warm with a gentle breeze. A few coins clinked together in her pocket. There was a hustle round the cart and then the crowd parted as Ruadhán strode across to hear of the merchant's news.

"What is the latest, my good man?" he said for all to hear.

The man removed his frayed bonnet and bowed his head. "There's trouble coming, my lord. You need to beware. A great mortality is coming this way and travelling fast, almost a mile and one quarter each day, so I'm told. I am going north as fast as I can and if I may have some bread and cheese I shall take to the road again with haste."

"Tell us, what does this mortality look like?" Ruadhán asked in the hush that followed.

"I haven't seen it, nor do I wish to. I hear it's a most dreadful plague and people are dying fast. Whole villages have succumbed. It's a fearful punishment from God. Pray, sir. Pray that He will save you and yours from this evil pestilence."

The crowd looked at one another and a hum of chatter spread as they contemplated this news and shared their fears. The poor merchant only made a few sales before everyone sought the safety of the familiar thick walls of the manor and its courtyard. Clémence, however, understood that walls would not keep out such a pestilence.

Ruadhán pondered on what he had heard from various sources, both in France and from the travelling merchant. He was uncharacteristic in his lack of action. He prevaricated constantly about Emma and Aedric. Was this a subconscious inclination of relief?

Clémence prompted him one day. "Are you going to fetch Lady Emma? If there is a plague coming, perhaps she should be here."

"Do you want me to ride out for her?" He watched as indecision flitted across her features, then he added, "If this Great Mortality is spreading as fast as I hear, we must put in place some measures to protect ourselves."

They spoke no more of it that day, but Ruadhán was less inclined to roam the country to fetch his errant intended. Many people's lives depended upon him. Finally, his conscience got the better of him and he prepared to travel to his uncle's manor to fetch Emma back. "After all, her father will not be impressed with me if I leave her to whatever lies ahead," he told Clémence.

While no further intimacy occurred between them, he realised he was relying increasingly on their brief conversations and he valued her opinion.

"It will take me two days each way and then some time at my uncle's manor. Do not let any strangers in while I am gone. Not even people who are familiar, for we know not what they may bring in the way of disease. I will instruct the men-at-arms and speak to Joan, too."

"I worry for my family," said Clémence.

"Of course. Perhaps we will need to bring people inside the moat to live here, if things appear to be as bad as they say."

Once his preparations were complete, Ruadhán came to find Clémence. She was in her solar. He had begun to think of it as hers, not Emma's. She leapt to her feet at his gentle tap on the open door.

"I am leaving now, but I shall return as soon as possible. I have no wish to stay longer that propriety demands."

"Safe travels." She took a step towards him, and all his resolve not to touch her disappeared. He reached out his hand and she stepped forward to take it.

"My love," he whispered, for he could deny it no longer.

Her eyes began to shine. "Don't, please. It's too difficult and you may yet be returning with Lady Emma."

"I know. I'm sorry. Keep safe and may God look upon us kindly." He could not resist cupping her cheek with his palm and his reward came when she leaned into his caress. He stepped away, before he lost himself completely.

The next five days were endless for Clémence. At the manor they saw no one else and although she could see some of the villagers working in fields from her window, no one came close. Word had spread and everyone was loath to intermingle. She longed to go to her home and speak with her father, but she could not.

Wandering in the garden, sewing, even practising her lettering, brought no satisfaction and Clémence found herself interminably bored. Her thoughts wound in an endless spiral and she began to imagine all ills befalling Ruadhán.

Clémence was looking out of her open window embrasure once more when she heard horses' hooves on the dried earth. Two riders were approaching from the north, and she recognised one instantly. He cut a fine figure as he rode at speed, his red hair flying behind him as he raised an arm to wave. Perhaps it was she he had spied and she raised her hand in return, a smile on her face. She waited and watched as the men opened the sturdy doors at his advance. He thundered over the bridge and dismounted, leaving a groom to see to the sweating animal. His attendant went to the stables. She flew down the stairs and met him in the hall.

"Tell me all. You are alone. Is all well? Is Lady Emma to follow? What of your journey?"

Ruadhán laughed. "So many questions. Wait while I have ale. It's thirsty work on the roads. They are dusty now the weather is so dry. Sit with me and I shall tell you all."

They sat either side of the fireplace. The logs were laid but there was no flame at this time of day and this season.

Ruadhán took a deep quaff from his mug. "I had a good journey, but when I arrived, Aedric's seneschal prevented me from seeing Lady Emma. My uncle was out riding in the forest, hunting. He was none too pleased to see me when he returned. He said I didn't trust him to take care of her. I assured him that was not the case, but since I had returned from the wars, her place was here, at the manor. Finally, I was able to see her. She looked pale and thin, but seemed well enough. She said she had had a sickness for some time, but that it had passed. We discussed this pestilence which seems to be coming and Aedric said she was safe where she was, with him, being further north than here. The lady herself said she would follow me here in a few days, when she has her strength back."

"That seems an amicable solution." Clémence was disappointed, but could see no way around the fact that Ruadhán and Emma were handfasted. "Perhaps I might go and see my family before Lady Emma returns?"

"Yes, certainly, but please do not go for long. I shall fear for you while you are away, and when you return, we must plan what to do to protect them and others should this Great Mortality arrive here, for I fear it surely will."

Clémence needed to distance herself from Ruadhán. He was not to be hers and the walk home would allow her time to think. When Emma returned, she had no doubt that they would be married, and she must decide if she could endure that. At one time she could, but now...?

"I want you to take someone with you," Ruadhán continued. "Perhaps the kitchen girl, Hawise. She has been unwell, I gather. I wondered if she might be of use to your mother, as I hear she had been finding it difficult to manage at home since the birthing of your brother."

Clémence was amazed that he taken the trouble to enquire after her mother, or was even aware of the pot-washer in his household. Surely this man was a rarity.

As they walked, Clémence was determined to find out what was wrong with Hawise, although she had an idea. Perhaps she could discern who the man was that had caused her to be with child. "Was it at Christmas when the bishop put you with John Bennett? Did you lie with him?" she asked gently.

The young woman hung her head and whispered. "No, it wasn't him. He was kind. We talked."

They walked on. Clémence decided to come straight to the point. "Who did you lie with, Hawise?"

Hawise wiped her eyes and sniffed. "I'll get into trouble," she whispered.

"No, you won't." They stopped walking and Clémence turned to Hawise. "No one will be cross and my mother will look after you, Hawise. Who was it?"

Her whisper was almost inaudible between her tears. "Sir Aedric."

Clémence sighed heavily. "All right, Hawise. My mother will look after you. I think you may be going to have a child."

Hawise's eyes widened. "But I don't want one," she said.

"I know, but we will share this with my family and tell them that Sir Ruadhán asks them to care for you. You will be able help my mother, since she too is unwell." Clémence hoped Catherine would take in this poor waif, for she had no one else.

At last they reached the Masson's home, where another shock awaited Clémence. Catherine was slumped in her chair. She looked drained and old as Clémence introduced Hawise, who stood inside the door. Clémence explained that Ruadhán would pay for Hawise to remain and be of service. She also told Caroline that the young woman might need her support in a few months' time. "Someone much older and should know better has taken advantage of her," she explained. Then, "I have brought you a ribbon, Mother. I weaved it myself on my lady's loom."

"You are a good girl," Catherine said, her voice weak.

At the midday meal her mother made a feeble attempt to eat some rabbit broth. Hawise leaned across from her place on the bench opposite, to help.

"Every effort seems to tire her, and the babe is weakening further," Agnes whispered later, as Catherine dozed before the fireplace. "Arthur has a flux and is not gaining weight as he should. We have tried soaking some bread in goat's milk and he will take some mashed carrot, but it's not enough to sustain him. I fear we shall lose him before long."

Clémence watched sadly as Hawise stroked Arthur's forehead as he slept in his bed box. She did not wish for her family to bury another child.

After lunch Clémence accompanied her father to the abbey. She was keen to see his sculptures and learn more of how the family were faring.

Her father gave a deep sigh. "Agnes has made up her mind. She is determined that she will only be happy when she had withdrawn entirely from the world, so that she may serve Almighty God worthily. She takes after her mother, who was a devout and quiet woman."

Clémence nodded. "She is determined to become a nun."

Merek shook his head. "No, dearest daughter. Not a nun. Agnes wishes to assume the hermit life. She will become an anchoress. Abbot Monkton at the Mother House has already made application on her behalf. He is petitioning the Bishop of Lincoln for her enclosure in a cell attached to our church."

"What? She will remain there? All the time?" Clémence was horrified.

"Yes, she will live a solitary life of prayer and contemplation."

Clémence had always known her sister wished for a pure life, but this! This was entirely different. To shut herself away in a narrow, cold and gloomy cell, never to see the sun shining on the cornfields, the frosty stars in the night sky, or the first feathering of green on the trees in the woods, and, worse still, to never to feel the warmth of a loving family, filled Clémence with dismay.

"What will happen next?"

"If her petition is considered kindly there will be a deputation from the clergy, who will question her closely regarding her sincerity, and also whether she has fully considered what she is doing in the service of God."

"Father, I know that Agnes has always been devout, but…" Clémence trailed off.

Seeing her agitation, Merek touched her shoulder. "Daughter, she will not be swayed."

"Does she go to the church? When last I was here she seemed less eager to visit on her own."

"Very rarely. She refuses to speak with Father Deodonatus and seems adamant in her desire."

Clémence could well understand why her sister would not wish to share her thoughts with a man who was so outrageously zealous in his views. She wished Father Robert were still here to counsel with kindness and wisdom.

"What of Mother? Does she know of Agnes' intention?"

"I have not shared it with her yet. She is not strong. I will wait to see what the clergy decide, first." He frowned and worry etched lines across his face.

When they arrived at the workshop, Clémence greeted her brother. "Mattie, my dear." She looked at his work. "You are doing very well, I hear, and now I see your work, I'm impressed."

"Really, Sister? It's good to see you." He grinned at her.

On the way home, Merek and Clémence talked about the great pestilence, since news was spreading. "Perhaps it won't reach us here in the country?" said her father.

Clémence was not so confident, and she determined to speak to Ruadhán about it once she returned to the manor.

She was awkward with her sister when they re-entered the house, having learned of Agnes' intention. Then there were the practical aspects of looking after the household. Increasingly she was grateful to Ruadhán for his suggestion that Hawise live with her parents, but who would feed her enclaved sister and deal with her daily personal issues? Would she rely on benevolence from the community to leave her food and empty her slops?

Clémence's journey home was uneventful. She was thankful not to have encountered Father Deodonatus and there had been no sign of Daniel for quite some time. As a result, she had been able to enjoy the spring birdsong and trees covered with luminous green among their branches.

When Clémence arrived back at the manor there was a flurry of activity on the road outside. An old woman in ragged clothes and sacking tied around her feet was shouting in an accent so strong that she could not identify it. She supported herself with a long straight branch and had a cloth bag slung over one shoulder. Her hair was grey and her weather-beaten face was a spider's web of wrinkles. As she shouted, she waved her stick about and her whole demeanour spoke of agitation.

"*Be woer!*" shouted the old woman, followed by "*Yfel!*" It sounded like 'beware' and 'evil', but Clémence couldn't be certain.

Ruadhán arrived and shooed everyone back to their work. As the workers scrambled back across the moat to address their tasks, he strode towards her with a smile.

"I'm pleased to see you," he said and Clémmie's heart gave a lurch.

Once more the woman shouted her warnings and they picked out the word *hearm*. Then she began an extraordinary mime while she shouted and waved her arms, something about *bweils* and *droat ha burst*. They picked out the word *cuman*.

"I think she's talking about this mighty pestilence about which we have heard," said Clémence. "She's talking of boils bursting at someone's throat, I believe. She says it's coming."

Ruadhán questioned the woman. Her speech was hard to discern but they gathered she spoke of fever and pain before pus-filled boils on necks, under arms and in groins caused death in a matter of days. There were whole villages where none survived. Lords were barring their gates to strangers but others were ill-prepared and suffered the consequences.

Ruadhán dug in his purse and gave her some coins. The woman wiped them on her clothing, then bit on one to verify its legitimacy before turning away with surprising speed. Ruadhán guided Clémence over the wooden bridge.

"Come, I would welcome your ideas about what we should do to protect ourselves and our people," he said.

Clémence and Ruadhán sat by the fire long into the night.

"I cannot believe that whole villages have sinned so badly that God would punish them all thus," she said.

"Me neither. Our people are not sinners to that extent. They do not commit grievous sins of lust, pride, and envy any more than the next. They do not murder, and gluttony is certainly not rife. Some may be slothful, but God would not punish us all in this way."

"I think it more likely that the pestilence is due to dirty living or something in the air, but if it spreads this fast, we must prepare. I think we should insist that everyone takes all slops away from dwellings. Perhaps I might show you what I had done soon after you left, my lord. The stream that runs behind the forge used to run into the moat, but I asked some of the men to build a bridge so it flows across it. It carries all the slops into the woods on the other side."

Ruadhán stared at her and Clémence wondered if she had over-stepped. "Whatever gave you the notion?"

"I have always done my lave away from the house where my parents live. I asked my father if he thought my idea would work and he suggested we line the trough which carries the water with clay, to ensure it does not leak. I thought it a good idea to stop effluent running into the moat. There were always rats there, but now there are hardly any."

"When the sun rises you must show me this invention." Ruadhán paused. "How might we protect those in the village? Perhaps we must encourage all to come and live inside the moat and we will burn the bridge. They could be here for some time, but we have stores to share."

"Food will be a concern for many. They must bring all their winter supplies and stocks. They will need clothing for an extended stay. How we will persuade them to come, I know not. It may be difficult for some to leave their homes. I mean, why would they believe us?"

"They are used to following my orders, of course, but I would that they choose to come under my protection."

Clémence stifled a yawn. It was well into the early hours and she had been up with the sunrise, having had a busy day and a long walk back to the manor. She decided not to share her worries about her sister. There were more pressing matters.

Clémence was awake and dressed before first light. When she descended the steps to the great hall, Ruadhán was already striding around restlessly. "Come, show me this work you had done," he said.

Together they walked across the courtyard, past the stables and then round to the barn. They continued towards the forge, the stone building set apart from the other wooden outbuildings. Behind, a stream, fed from somewhere beyond the undulating low hills that rose behind the demesne, had originally flowed away through the woods and towards the flat lands of the Fens. Ancestors from the days of the first King William had dug the moat and encouraged part of the stream to flow into it, allowing the rest to course its way through the manor grounds, before finding the moat again and disappearing beyond to the flat lands. Now, with Clémence's moderation, instead of flowing back into the moat as it exited the grounds, it entered a trough supported by sturdy oak posts which rose from small stone buttresses sitting in the moat.

Ruadhán looked impressed. "You've thought of everything. The stones will protect the posts so that they don't rot and break, and the clay lining prevents any effluent from leaking away too soon."

"My father suggested the clay. The men were not happy with me when I insisted on seasoned wood. Oak is valuable, I know, and I'm sorry if I asked too much."

"It is perfect for a long-standing construction, such as this. If we want others, to sustain more people living within the manor grounds, and the stream is big enough, we could use green wood for those. Hopefully, they will not need to be in use for long. I shall get some men onto it at once."

"If many more people are to live here, perhaps the hospital house which the monks maintain might give advice," suggested Clémence. "After all, they help the poor and sick pilgrims that pass."

"That's a good idea. I shall visit the abbey and speak to them about their preparations. They will not want to close their doors, I'm sure, and will probably continue to administer to the community. Though I fear they will suffer as a result."

"Will you ride again to the Lady Emma?" Clémence asked.

Ruadhán shook his head. "I will ask one of the sokemen to go on my behalf if she doesn't return soon. I could send my signature on a parchment. Aedric doesn't read so my messenger will have to tell him the communiqué. I'll leave it a few days. Lady Emma said she would follow when she regained her strength."

Clémence wondered whether to suggest she might be with child, or perhaps had lost a babe, but decided against it. She had no proof that Aedric would treat Lady Emma as he had done Hawise.

"I would like you to accompany me to visit the monks," Ruadhán said, interrupting her thoughts.

Clémence hesitated. "What will people say? I am a humble servant of Lady Emma."

"You have more intelligence and innovative ideas than most here. Anyway, it is no one's business but ours, where we go."

They rode out together that afternoon. The sun was strong, shining on the creamy stones of the building which rose ahead of them. The unadorned Cistercian style had a purity of design that was simple and moving, and was surrounded by ancient trees.

"I have received this communication," Abbot Walter said, as they seated themselves in the small inner parlour. "I thought it must be serious to have received it in writing." He opened a small scroll and sat looking at it with a frown on his face.

Ruadhán prompted him. "Does it relate to the great pestilence to which I referred?"

"Oh yes. Yes indeed." He paused again. "It has come from our Lord Archbishop of York himself, but complications delayed its arrival. The Archbishop of Canterbury was to write it, but he has succumbed, and so the task landed with the prior of Christchurch in Canterbury and sent widely from there."

"The Archbishop had the plague?" Ruadhán's expression was one of shock.

"I know not if that was the cause, but let me read some of this to you." Abbot Walter cleared his throat and began to read: "*A catastrophic and deadly pestilence increases in its severity since its arrival and has spread across a neighbouring kingdom.*" He looked up at the two of them. "Our own Bishop writes '*unless we pray devoutly and incessantly the pestilence will stretch its poisonous branches into this realm and strike down and consume its residents so we will do all that we can. And then we can do no more and God will determine.*' When we bless the holy bread all who consume it shall have health in body as well as of the soul. Those who die with sins unconfessed and who are unrepentant will go to Hell, so we shall continue with our work, Sir Ruadhán."

131

"I think it will take more than prayer this time, Father," said Ruadhán. "I propose to close confine my manor house, and to encourage the local people to join me there. Would you lend one of your number to us for the duration, so that our souls will not suffer?"

Clémence sent a silent prayer that it would not be Father Deodonatus. Then inspiration struck. "Perhaps one of your more mature members, Father? Someone who cannot walk too far in the ministrations across the demesne. After all, the confines of the manor house would not be too difficult for such a one."

"You are right, my child." Abbot Walter smiled at her beatifically.

"I shall send word when we have spoken to our community and when we are ready to burn the bridge. Perhaps you might keep your own counsel on this matter. We do not want to cause panic," Ruadhán said.

"Of course. Now, let me give you my blessing."

Clémence glanced at Ruadhán as they both knelt before the old prior. He gave her his gentle smile and a frisson of pleasure ran through her body. She tried to concentrate as the priest closed his eyes and raised his right hand, but all she could think of was Ruadhán's close proximity and all she could hear was his breathing.

CHAPTER 14

Clémence was working on a new panel of the embroidery. Although she had disliked the activity at first, when she was searching her mind for something to occupy Lady Emma all those months ago, now she found solace in the story she was creating. Her needle poised when she heard footsteps on the stairs, before there was knock at the door.

It was Ruadhán. He waved a small piece of parchment at her.

"What is this?" he demanded. "Your sister wishes to become an anchoress? Why did you not say? The Bishop of Lincoln commands me to attend a meeting with him and his priests at St Michael's church next week, where they will question her and those around her as to her sobriety and suitability."

Clémence stood. Her eyes pricked as she tried to deny the tears that welled at his tone. "There is so much to worry over and consider here. I wished not to trouble you further, my lord."

"I thought we were friends. How could you have said nothing until it's almost too late."

Friends? Is that all they were? But of course. How could it ever be more. Clémence dipped a curtsey. "Sire, Ruadhán, of course we are … friends." She cleared her throat. "I didn't wish to worry you more, that is all."

"We'll go to this meeting! You will come too." He turned and stalked away.

Alone again, her tears fell, uncontrolled. The situation was bad enough without his attitude towards her. How could she bear it? She flung herself onto the bed, using the cushions to deaden the sound, she howled her anger and frustration, crying until her eyes were red and swollen.

Over the next few days Ruadhán rode around the village and outlying hamlets to speak with the householders about the plans for their protection from the coming plague. Clémence watched him go from the upstairs window, before turning her attention with lacklustre enthusiasm back to her embroidery. On one occasion he demanded that she accompany him, claiming that she would know better how to approach some of the serfs, not because he wanted her company Thinking back, perhaps he had never fostered more, and it had all been in her wishful imagination.

"You are their overlord. They must do as you say," she said, without heart.

"Yes, but if they come to us willingly, the enforced time together in close confinement will be easier to manage." Then he added, "If our Lord de Beaumont was resident at Folkingham, I would have to defer all the decisions to him, but since he is at one of his other castles, I am determined to make our own preparations and save ourselves and my loyal tenants."

"That's wise, certainly. If we delay or await his decisions, we may perish. The letter from the archbishop was clear."

Conversation was strained, focussing on facts, and they rode for some without speaking at all.

"There is still no sign of Lady Emma's return." Ruadhán sighed. "It will take too long to ride all that way again."

Clémence made no further comment for several minutes, but she couldn't resist giving her opinion, even if he hadn't sought it. "You could send a messenger? One of your free tenants, perhaps. You spoke of the suggestion before, I believe."

"Yes, indeed. At least I shall have done my best by her and those with whom she resides. I shall send Joseph Mercer. He is trustworthy. He will convey my meaning honestly."

They rode on in silence for a while longer before Ruadhán spoke again. "We are approaching your home. I should like to visit there with you and encourage your family to join us at the manor. I would not have you worry for them and I most certainly do not want you to feel obliged to join them and to put yourself at risk."

Clémence was grateful for the sentiment though the atmosphere was still strained. It must suit his purpose for her to remain at the manor, especially if Lady Emma were to return. It had been in her mind that perhaps she should leave her employ and return home to care for her family.

Ruadhán dismounted and knocked on the door. Her father opened it and smiled broadly until he saw his lord's expression, and then his own countenance froze. "Sire, there is a problem?"

"Indeed there is, or there will be, soon," replied Ruadhán.

"Come in, please. Daughter, it is good to see you." Merek hastily embraced Clémence before turning to the interior. "Wine for our guest."

Hawise hastily dropped her spindle and hurried to comply.

Agnes and Catherine bobbed curtseys to the lord of the manor.

Once all were seated around the table, with Ruadhán accepting her father's normal place at the head, he spoke. "There is a great peril coming. I have heard from the Lord Archbishop, and the king himself has sent messengers around the country. Others have told me tales of horror and suffering. A pestilence like no other is spreading across the land and we must do all we can to save ourselves."

"We have heard similar stories," Merek said, looking concerned.

"God is sending a terrible punishment," Agnes said.

"God, or people's insanitary or unclean habits that welcome rats to the thatch of their houses," Clémence muttered.Ruadhán continued. "I want all who are able to enter my manor premises and stay until the pestilence has passed, as it surely will. We must gather all our resources to store and share. We will construct shelters in the grounds around the manor house and then destroy the bridge over the moat to prevent wandering people who may come to steal what we have or inadvertently spread the pestilence."

"Is this truly necessary?"

"I am certain of it."

"Then we are indebted to you, sir," Merek said.

Agnes suddenly stood and stepped away from the table. "I will not be coming," she said, "though I thank you for your kind offer, sir."

"Daughter, you must come." Merek reached out towards her.

Agnes raised her hands, palms out towards him to arrest his movement and shook her head. "You know I have another plan and God will protect me when he sees my devotion is pure."

"I understand the meeting is next week for the decision by the clergy," Ruadhán said. "I am summoned. I know you are chaste and devout, Mistress Masson, but this idea of yours, it—"

"Sister, please," Clémence interrupted. "I beg you to rethink. Especially at this time of peril. Please!"

"I cannot. It is my calling."

Clémence's throat seemed to be closing and tears stung her eyes. Then she thought of a winning argument. "But who will feed you if we are at the manor? You will starve and then there will be no prayers to help."

Catherine gasped and clutched her chest as she nodded.

"Those who are left, and there will be some, will serve me," replied Agnes. "The monks will donate some bread and ale, and empty my pot. Of this I am certain. I shall be spared any pestilence with my prayers for us all, and my contemplations of the scriptures. Do not fear for me, for I do not." Agnes made the sign of the cross and whispered, "Amen."

Hawise, who had remained standing beside the fireplace, sniffed noisily. All eyes turned to her. Her small swell of her belly was clear now for all to see.

"You may come, too," Ruadhán said. "I know you are with child."

Hawise sniffed again and bobbed a curtsey.

Clémence looked at Ruadhán in admiration. Despite her hurt at his comment about them being just 'friends', her appreciation of his forward-thinking and his generous deeds only served to increase her admiration for him. Her heartache intensified and her sense of injustice at the difference in their positions escalated. A single tear rolled down her cheek and she dashed it away while the room looked at Hawise.

John Gyndwelle, the Bishop of Lincoln, sat on a grand chair before the altar. Formerly Archdeacon of Northampton, he had been appointed bishop six years previously, and thus was highly experienced in church business. He had with him two deacons of the diocese.

Gyndwelle was an imposing figure. Over his white alb, with its elaborately embroidered cuffs and hem, he wore his dalmatic, deliberately ornate with costly adornment to impress, which it did. Because he had travelled, the mozetta around his shoulders was fashioned from thick wool dyed red, and now the hood hung down his back. His pectoral cross of gold hung around his neck and rested on his chest, so all might realise his special powers.

One of the deacons stood at his side, holding the crozier of office. The tall bishop's mitre, with its intricate and symbolic embroidery, sat on a small table to his side.

As other invitees arrived, they knelt to kiss the single large ruby on the bishop's ring, before taking their allotted seats in order of seniority. Abbot Walter, from the monastery at Grimsthorpe, sat next to the bishop, with Father Deodonatus, as the monk collaborating most closely with the people of the demesne, beside him. Ruadhán took his place on the far side of the bishop's entourage.

Clémence and her parents, along with Ruadhán and the people of the manor, who had been given leave to attend, gradually filled the rest of the space. The church was full and people spilled from the doors into the graveyard beyond, such was the level of curiosity. The community wanted to know what would happen. While adults clustered together to hear messages passed from those closest to the doors, children chased across grassy mounds and played leapfrog since, although a solemn occasion, it was also an unexpected holiday.

A hush fell as Agnes entered the church. Her head was down, her hands clasped in front of her, and her lips moved slightly as she walked. She was dressed in a dark shift with an equally plain kirtle, enhancing the slightness of her figure and making her face look sallow and thin. There was a fresh breeze and the day was unseasonably cold. Clémence could see strain in Agnes's expression and thought she must be freezing, though she could see she wasn't shivering. Her face showed strong determination.

If only she would recant, Clémence thought, but in the next moment she knew that Agnes would not. Clémence prayed that Agnes would not come to regret this decision in the long hours of her seclusion.

Agnes knelt before their lordships and made her confession public. Her sins, as she described them, were so simple and minor. She outlined her impatience with the new maid, Hawise, for some careless spinning. She allowed a stock pot to boil over, and she made a sharp remark to their brother, Mattie, when he was late for supper. Clémence knew her own sins of yearning for a man beyond her reach were far greater. All could hear her sister given absolution.

The questions began. "Are you Agnes, daughter of Merek Masson, master stonemason in this parish?"

"I am."

"Are you single, or espoused to anyone, or joined in matrimony, or have you ever been?"

"I am single, Father, and virginal." Agnes spoke with clarity and her voice carried to all who listened.

Father Deodonatus looked at Agnes. Even at this distance Clémence could see his eyes glittering with his own fanaticism. "You have made humble petition to John Gyndwelle, our most noble Lord, the Bishop of Lincoln, to grant you a licence to remove yourself and spend the remainder of your life in all sincerity, sanctity and chastity in an enclosed space within the precincts of this church. Is this so?"

"I have."

Bishop Gyndwelle recommenced his questions. "Why do you wish to do this, my child?"

"So I may serve Almighty God more worthily through prayer and meditation, abandoning all worldly things and strive towards the fulfilment of a better life."

"If I grant your petition, will you make a solemn vow in this place, before me and before God, for all to hear, that you will remain in the narrow place that will be constructed for you, in perpetual continence, and chastity, even to your life's natural end?"

The silence in the church was absolute. They all awaited the response. Then Agnes answered in a whisper, "I will."

A collective exhalation passed around the church.

Clémence took Catherine's hand as tear ran down her cheek. Agnes had not raised her eyes to those who interrogated her, but had kept her gaze to the floor. She looked fragile and drained of all healthy colour.

"Who will speak first with regard to the life and conduct of this maid?" The bishop's deep voice rang out. "Who will say whether she is likely to succeed in this saintly proposal she is undertaking? Will she keep her vow? Speak out."

Father Deodonatus stood. "I shall speak.

Agnes' eyes shot up to look at him before returning to gaze at the stones on which she knelt.

As her parish priest, I say she adheres to religious teachings, she accepts the Holy Host with regularity at her home or here in this church. I know her to be devout."

Clémence could discern none of the passionate fanaticism that she had witnessed before from the priest, but his eyes looked hooded as he stared down upon her sister. She did not trust him.

Others followed and spoke of Agnes' humility, her dutiful and devout observance. They vouched for her purity, her strength of belief, and her determination to fulfil her vow.

Finally, Bishop Gyndwelle beckoned for one of his deacons to place his mitre on his head. He looked even taller and more imposing when he stood. He took his crozier in his own hand. He indicated for Agnes to rise.

"Raise your eyes, my child, that I may see into them and read your soul. I have much experience of the human condition and have looked into many pairs of eyes before." His voice carried to the far walls. "There are those that are bright with religious fervour. Some are sullen and others rebellious. I have seen serenity and the comfort of genuine belief. There are those that slide from mine, filled with guilt." He bent to look at Agnes and then spoke so softly that only those close by could hear.

Clémence strained to hear his words.

"I'm unsure of candour in your gaze. It's reserved and steady, certainly, but I have a distinct impression of a deep and secret inner pain."

"Your lordship, I have contemplated this well, and was questioned about it by my mother and dear sister as well as others." Agnes glanced across at Clémence and Catherine. "But I have considered this course for many years and see no other choice for me."

The bishop turned to Merek. "It is you who will construct this cell, inside the church wall?"

"Yes, sir. Over there." Merek pointed to the north wall. "The cell will be six feet by ten feet, as advised. I propose a small door so that she may receive gifts of food and drink, and take the sacrament, too. There will be a squint window that she might regard the altar and take comfort from the sight."

"Very good. You understand this walling in represents death to the world for an anchorite such as she, and the only way forward is towards Heaven?"

"Yes, your lordship."

"Ensure the floor has a pit for her grave."

"Yes, sir."

Clémence shuddered and looked across at Ruadhan with tears staining her cheeks.

"Then, before you all, as witness to her vow and to this act, I grant permission for this maid to take sanctuary. As soon as the enclave is ready the monks of Grimsthorpe abbey will escort her therein, to spend the rest of her natural life in piety and prayer. It will be the responsibility of all to give her basic sustenance that she might fulfil this desire of Almighty God." He made the sign of the cross over the whole gathering and there was a muted "Amen".

As the crowd began to disperse, Father Deodonatus stepped forward, his hands clasped together and his head bowed. "Sire, before you go, I would bring a matter to your attention. In the very same house that the pious young maid has been residing, there is another who is not so pure. It is a matter for my conscience that I speak."

"That is a manorial matter, Father," Abbot Walter said. "Now is not the time. Perhaps we might see the Lord Bishop on his way. He has had a most tiring day and he has far to go." He turned to Ruadhán. "Sir, might we convene at the Masson's cottage and have a short discussion before you return to the manor house?"

"Indeed, Father."

They arranged the details of their meeting and parted ways. Ruadhán glared at Father Deodonatus as he left the church and Merek Masson rounded up his family, to return home.

As she and Ruadhán walked towards her parents' house, Clémence was silent. She took no joy in the bird song or the wildflowers that peppered the verges. Her thoughts were of Agnes, but now there was the added worry of Father Deodonatus and his self-righteous indignation of Hawise living in the same house. Yet the young woman was largely blameless. How could she have possibly stood against Sir Aedric?

As they approached the dwelling, they could saw Hawise sitting outside at her loom, despite the frigid air. She dropped the spindle on the stone beside her and leaped to her feet, pressing her lean body against the wall, and dropping her chin to her chest.

"Are you coming inside, Hawise?" Clémence asked. "It's cold today. You need not stay outside."

"No, mistress, I'd best get on." She dropped a deep curtsey as Ruadhán passed through the door. "You go in, Miss."

It wasn't long before Abbot Walter and Father Deodonatus followed. Clémence poked her head out of the door at the sound of a pony's hooves and saw Hawise's skirts disappearing round the corner of the cottage as she scuttled away from greeting the monastic gentlemen. Father Deodonatus led the pony and when they arrived at the door Abbot Walter used the stone seat to dismount.

Catherine served the guests refreshments. She bustled to the best of her ability, determined to assume her role, as it wasn't often that such a learned and important figure as Abbot Walter graced their home.

"I'm sure we can deal with this matter swiftly," Abbot Walter said.

Father Deodonatus cleared his throat. "This woman, Hawise Webb, has sinned. It is a serious matter. I think we should discuss the leyrwite. This hundred-year-old fine for engaging in fornication is due to the lord of the manor, for she will be a burden on our community. At the very least, we should insist she pays her dues."

Clémence was certain the monk was enjoying every moment of his speech encouraging payment from Hawise for her sin.

His obsequious manner, as he stood next to his senior was disturbing.

Abbot Walter grunted. "And in all that time there have been less that fifty cases of the leyrwite being paid, and always it has fallen on our poorest people."

Father Deodonatus mumbled his response. "Yes, because otherwise they need supporting when they cannot work. It should be any amount from six pence to four shillings but it might go some way to recompense."

Clémence heard a scurrying outside and wondered if Hawise had crept back to listen.

"May I say something, Father?" Clémence stepped forwards.

"Yes, child."

She glanced at Ruadhán before speaking. "Hawise is a poor waif. She could not afford to pay anything, and she has told me that she was an unwilling participant."

"Did she say who this fellow was?"

"Not directly." It was not her place to name Sir Aedric. That a servant such as she would castigate a lord may not be tolerated.

Ruadhán spoke out. "Hawise was under my roof and so some of the responsibility for her protection rests with me. I do not demand leyrwite from her. She could not pay, anyway. What say you, Master Masson?"

"The lass may reside here and help my wife, who, as you know, is not strong. When the babe is born, we shall decide more. I agree, she will not be able to pay leyrwite."

"But —" began Father Deodonatus.

"No, Father. The decision is mine and Sir Ruadhán's to make, not yours." Abbot Walter was adamant. "Fetch the girl here. There will be no dues paid and she may reside here. I shall tell her."

Father Deodonatus bowed and turned to the door. He looked out. "She is not there."

Merek squeezed past and looked around the corner, before returning. "Indeed she is nowhere to be seen. Shall I speak with her in regard to your decision when she returns? I am sure that won't be long. It's cold today and will be dark before long."

Hawise had still not returned by the time Clémence and Ruadhán left for the manor. At the door, hurried words between the two sisters still did not change Agnes' mind, for she refused to forego her vow. "It is done," she said. "It is what I want."

"But it will be cold and dank. There may be rats," Clémence said.

I shall have a candle at my door. Nothing will get in. I have decided, Sister." She took a deep breath. "I look forward to the peace and safety of the cell." She glanced over her shoulder at the monastery visitors and Clémence wondered anew of what Agnes referred.

"What of this pestilence that is coming and of which everyone is talking?"

"Enough, Sister. I have made my choice."

Ruadhán glanced across at Clémence as they rode to the manor. His heart ached for their lost companionship and he blamed himself. He had been hurt that she had not confided in him sooner with regard to her sister's wish and had reacted in anger. "The monks will ensure Agnes has a fresh pitcher of water each day and her pail emptied. They will give her bread, perhaps a fish or two from their pond." He paused. "It is her choice. She has always been devout."

Clémence fixed her gaze on the path ahead.

He said no more and wished them back at the manor so he might find his own solace within a cup of wine and think about how he might make this better. He decided to hide behind practical issues.

"I must work the men hard to complete the dwellings for the villagers to join us within the safety of our moat, and they must complete the sanitary arrangements to the rear of the manor. I'll ride out tomorrow and ensure that all we require is collected and brought in. If this Great Mortality is as bad as we think, then we must prepare with all haste."

There was silence from his companion.

"I expect to hear any day now from my lord uncle's demesne with regard to Lady Emma's progress. Perhaps she will accompany my messenger and return."

"Perhaps she will."

It was almost dark when Ruadhán's sturdy mount and the pony Clémence rode clipped across the wooden bridge over the moat. Soon, that same crossing would be destroyed for their protection and they would be trapped together for who knew how long while they waited for the pestilence to pass.

As they crossed the bridge, Clémence was desperate for the warmth of his arms around her shoulders, for the feel of his lips upon hers. Somehow, they must find a way to return to their easy companionship, although if Lady Emma was to return, that would be impossible.

As soon as she had handed her reins to a groom, she hurried indoors and retreated to the solar. At the top of the stairs, she risked a look down and saw Ruadhán with a deep scowl before he turned from her and walked to the fire at the far end of the great hall. She heard him call for wine, and wretchedness overtook her. This placement had held so much promise, and now it seemed an atonement for her sin of wishing herself better than she was.

She hoped that by now Hawise had returned to her parents' home and been reassured that her immediate future was secure. At least that was one less worry.

CHAPTER 15

Two weeks passed before Clémence returned to the church at Edenham. It was with heavy despondency, for this was the day Agnes was to be enclaved. When she arrived, she saw the completed cell, with the squint so that her sister might view the altar, and a small port at the bottom of the stout door through which she could pass out her pail and receive basic sustenance. Above that was a grill with iron bars.

Would she embroider this moment into her frieze? That was for debate within her own soul. She tried not to envisage the long hours of solitude and the emotional coldness of the lonely cell that Agnes was about to face. Her own desires for Ruadhán and the impossibility of her feelings for him only seemed more implausible next to her sister's selfless act. Then again, was Agnes being completely selfless? Surely she was retreating from the world in which she could be doing so much good for others, not least her own family. Clémence castigated herself for having such thoughts when the community was saying payers and celebrating this act as one of extreme devotion to God.

The church was cold, but the service short. Clémence watched as Agnes entered the cell and the door closed with a dull, deep thud.

"I have done my best to ensure Agnes will be safe and have as much space as possible within the regulations for confinement," said Merek, afterwards. "Now, your mother needs to be taken home with all speed."

Clémence could see that Catherine was visibly upset. "Where is Hawise?" she asked, glancing around.

"There has been no sign of her since Abbot Walter came to the house. I can only assume she has returned to her own village and pray to God she is safe."

Clémence was troubled and thought to ask Ruadhán to send out a search party.

"Come, we must return to the manor house," he said, as he came to her side.

"I wondered…" She shook her head, hesitating to ask another favour of him when all was so tense and there was so much to be done. She left her request regarding Hawise unsaid.

"All will be ready for you to move your household to safety soon," he added, turning to Merek.

As the days passed, small dwellings appeared on the meadow inside the moat and on the paddocks. In the manor's orchard, the community erected more. Children and the elderly were offered accommodation in the great hall, where the servants slept. Sheep grazed in the graveyard, among the stones. Preserved vegetables, meats, and fruits were stored in the kitchen and pantry, from where they would be distributed with fairness. The barns and stables contained grain and other cereals.

Some chose to remain in their own homes and tend the fields. Ruadhán allowed the sokemen this privilege, but all serfs were commanded. He issued a statement to all the servants that they could stay or return to their families. Sir Ruadhán was uncompromising in his view of protecting the workers in his community.

Gossip was rife when the messenger, Joseph Mercer, returned from Sir Aedric's manor.

He rushed to Ruadhán to convey his news. "My lord, Lady Emma will not come. She professes illness. Sir Aedric said he will return here as soon as possible, even if it means leaving her behind. He is afeared, like many others."

Ruadhán grunted. "If he does not arrive imminently, he will be too late. I shall not wait. Is it the pestilence that sweeps the continent that has Lady Emma in its grasp? Has it come already?"

"No, my lord, it is not, but I have this to tell, too. I have witnessed the plague itself." Ruadhán took a step back. "I did not go near, sir. It was several days ago and I have not been unwell since. I have avoided all habitation since and I would not risk bringing it here."

"Where was this? Tell me all that you know."

"I passed by a village where a man was lying. None would go near him. I shouted to the priest who was there, but I did not go near. No one knows the cause. The priest said it was a punishment from God. Others said it was an odorous miasma. Perhaps it is true that the air is corrupt, and there is a disturbance of the elements. We should concentrate on balancing the body's humours.""Did you see the afflicted?"

"Only from a distance, sir. He lay outside on a pallet. It was truly horrid." Joseph made the sign of the cross to protect himself. "The man had black pustules on his neck. The priest said there were others in his groin and armpits. The whole village needed burning, I'd say. I've never seen so many rats."

"We must send to all the people to come now and seal the manor," Ruadhán said decisively. "You have done well, Joseph. Go and wash yourself and get some food from the kitchens."

Within two days the manor house had become a fortress, with no room to spare. Over a hundred people had arrived. Space was cramped, with villagers and their belongings taking up every available corner. Clémence shared her quarters in Lady Emma's solar with several other higher-ranking servants.

People crammed into the great hall, all lying within touching distance, while families moved into the single-room dwellings, constructed in haste. There wasn't enough thatch for the roofs, so overlapping planks of wood kept out the weather. This was less inclined to house rats, which always lived within the thatch of the cottages in the village.

Word spread quickly of the scene that Joseph Mercer had witnessed and those who had chosen to come were happy enough for the time being, trusting in the good advice of their lord. How long this would last, Ruadhán and Clémence did not know. The watery boundary that the moat provided protected everyone inside it. Trusted men would destroy the bridge, and all inside were forbidden to leave once it had been fired.

In the new year, everyone gathered to watch the burning of the bridge. The heat was intense once the faggots were set alight and the old dry wood of the structure had caught. They all watched as the fields beyond the manor, from which they had harvested all their crops, were lost to a handful of people who had refused to join them. There would be insufficient to prepare and seed the land in the spring. Hectares of good production would be impossible for the few who were left outside, but not within reach of those inside the moat.

Clémence thought of Agnes alone in her cell and wondered where Hawise had gone. She sat for long, lonely hours in her room, only occasionally sewing, and her nights were restless. One night she was looking out of her window when she thought she saw movement below. She strained forwards and as the moon broke from the clouds, she thought she saw two figures.

Ruadhán stood in the shadows and watched as Joan spoke with the kitchen boy. She was piling cheese and bread onto a cloth, which she tied with the four corners. "You tell no one, you hear?"

"No, missus. I'll say nought. What will I say anyhow?"

"You'll not say you saw me here this night and certainly not what I have here. If you do, the plague will come for you, and you'll die a horrible, painful death. Do you hear me?"

The boy took a step backwards, looking at her with frightened eyes.

She left him cowering and hurried away. Ruadhán let her go. If she didn't want to stay, he couldn't begrudge her a little food after her years of loyal service.

He followed her silently and stood in the shadows of the manor wall. The stars were few and clouds scurried across the night sky. A shadow left the far side of the barn and, joining it, Joan slid silently to the rear of the manor house.

With a faint *splosh*, the crude raft launched into the moat. Joan sat in the middle with her bags. It wobbled precariously as a man stepped upon it.

"Take care, you oaf. You'll have us both in," Ruadhán heard Joan hiss, her voice carrying on the night air.

"It's only made from leftover pieces of the roof planking, but it'll do," the man said. "We'll be fine and right soon enough."

"I'll go to a friend's and you may do as you please, Daniel."

"I'm grateful to you for taking me in and hiding me these past weeks. Living rough in the woods has been no festival, but I don't take to being a prisoner here either. Now, let's say no more until we reach the other side and away." He concentrated on 'rowing' with a plank of wood, as he stood at the back of the raft.

It took a while but at last the front of the makeshift craft stuck fast in the mud on the far bank. Joan tossed her bags onto the grass before pulling up her skirt to scramble after them, her hands pulling on the tufted turf.

Daniel followed, putting his broad shoulders to hauling the craft onto the bank. With a last look over his shoulder he said, "I see there's no longer hope for me and Agnes, though I might decide to hang around for a while to make sure she is all right. The woods will give me shelter away from everyone. I'm used to that. Then I'll disappear, probably up to Scotland or somewhere far away." He waved Joan goodbye before heading into the woods.

Clémence had listened from her place on the bank. When she had seen the shadows from her window, she had hurried outside on silent feet. There was no point in stopping them. If they wanted to go, so be it. She was surprised that Daniel had been back, but relieved that he would ensure Agnes was safe before he left again. He had hidden loyalties, it would seem. She turned to make her way back indoors and was startled as another shadow approached.

"What are you doing out here?" Ruadhán asked.

"I couldn't sleep and I saw two people —"

"I know. It was Joan. Daniel Farmer helped her to leave. The kitchen boy told me. He had not the wit to raise the alarm and was too frightened at first to tell anyone that she threatened him with plague if he told anyone before morning. Perhaps I should go after them."

"You have set the rules for everyone. You can hardly break them."

"I would do that if it made you happier," he said. "I hate to see you so sorrowful. These past weeks have been hard for everyone but you are carrying an extra burden."

Clémence looked up into his eyes. She saw the familiar spark and, unbidden, her heart beat faster. "It's not safe. Remember?"

He placed his forefinger beneath her chin and raised her face to his. "I remember many things. Not least the kiss we shared right here that Christmas."

"I remember it too, but we are not the same, you and I. I am a servant and you are a king's knight."

Ruadhán shook his head. "I am simply a man and you are the one I love."

Clémence gulped. This must not be. Lady Emma might yet return, and besides, she did not wish to go to Hell, or worse, remain in purgatory for a sin into which such as this could turn. She turned in a daze and stumbled for the door. She didn't stop. She hurtled up the stairs and into the solar where, with her back pressed to the closed door, she stood breathing heavily. Footsteps sounded and paused outside the chamber. Clémence tensed and after a moment the sound of steps on the rushes moved away. She took a deep breath. Lying on the bed at last, tears came. She didn't know who she was crying for. It could have been for Hawise, or for Agnes, but then she realised it was for herself.

Now Clémence had a new role and one that left her no time for self-pity. It was a massive task to organise the household; plan the food, ensuring supplies were not depleted too quickly; keep all safe; and make certain morale was as high as possible under the difficult circumstances. She fell into bed at night exhausted and slept until she heard the bells ring for Lauds. Daylight didn't break until well after the monks rang Prime. She prayed for them and their health as she set about her daily tasks. God would look after them, surely, and keep the pestilence at bay. They were giving her sister food and drink. They must survive.

One morning Ruadhán came to seek her out in the kitchens and Clémence realised she hadn't seen him for several days.

"Come, I would speak with you," he said.

She followed him outside to a quiet corner of the orchard. It was still early and few were awake and about. Chilly all of a sudden, Clémence pulled her shawl closer around her shoulders.

Her heart thumped with anticipation yet she was afraid that it might be some further catastrophe, so keeping her distance, she tried to close her mind and put off what he had to say.

"I went to Edenham church yesterday evening."

He had her full attention. Clémence was shocked at his foolhardiness. "What? You left the manor?"

"Shh! Keep your voice down," Ruadhán hissed. "Your sister Agnes is all right. The monks are making sure she is well cared for, although some of them have succumbed to the pestilence. Others in the village have caught it, too."

Unconsciously, Clémence took a step back from him.

"I have been sheltering out there, for several days. I have not succumbed to the disease. I burned rosemary for protection and stayed away from others. I washed each day in the river. And see? Here I am, safe and healthy."

Clémence stared at him. "You did that for me?"

"Yes, I did."

Tears filled her eyes and she was unable to prevent them tumbling down her cheeks. Her voice came as a whisper. "Thank you."

Ruadhán stepped towards her and wiped her tears away with his thumb. "There is one more thing. It's about Hawise. I saw

Caleb Snuggs in the fields and he shouted across to me. He has news of her, but it's not good."

Clémence took a deep breath and waited to hear.

"He found her under the willow tree near the bridge, floating among the reeds by the riverbank. There were no marks of violence upon on her, except a bruise on her side. Father Deodonatus declared it was a suicide and her body buried outside the precincts of the church in an unmarked grave."

Clémence gasped and crossed herself. "God bless her soul," she whispered. "Surely it may not be a suicide. She would have thought of her child. Her condition was not her fault. She should have no blame."

"No, it was not of her making, and I am deeply sorry. When all this is over, she shall have a place here in our graveyard."

That awful man, Aedric, should pay. It was his fault, Clémence thought.

CHAPTER 16

Clémence was sitting in a corner of the great hall. The weather was chill and one of the servants had recently heaved two logs from the *stère* onto the fire. The one metre lengths would last for a while, and the wood burned brightly in the massive grate. The warmth was welcome. The small group of children at Clémence's feet gazed up at her with earnest expressions as she tried to make her teaching fun. She remembered how Father Robert had enthused her as a child and how her mind had soaked up all the learning he could provide.

The peace of the afternoon was suddenly fractured by a muffled cry from outside. One child clung to Clémence's skirts, while others turned to each other in fear, having only half understood the peril they faced when overhearing adults as they discussed things in concerned whispers. Another shout was heard, joined by yet more calls. Clémence stood and the children scattered.

Someone opened the door and the wind blew in, lifting some of the rushes and bringing a scattering of dried brown leaves. She heard the hooves of riders and the harsh sounds of men calling as they approached. Rushing outside with others, Clémence stood looking across the moat towards the untended fields.

"I was afraid of this," Ruadhán said at her side.

She hadn't heard his approach and as she looked up at him, she saw the lines of worry etched deep into his forehead. She had kept away from him as much as she could, although it was impossible not to see him around the manor house and its grounds when they all lived together in close confinement.

"Someone has heard of our continuing fortunes here, that we have food and the people are protected," he said. Then, "I recognise that horse, but I do not know the rider."

Even Clémence knew the black courser belonged to a nobleman. "It looks like six riders, but one is slumped in his saddle."

"Indeed. We cannot allow them to come in."

"It does not bode well, I fear."

Someone in the crowd whispered, "Surely our lord will grant them access. It would be cruel not to."

Clémence turned to see Marie standing nearby. *She is as thoughtless as ever*, she thought to herself.

Further mutterings rolled around. Ruadhán turned and spoke. "There is no cure for this pestilence. I protect you here and you have not seen all the devastation and pain, as have I. Let me remind you." He described the suffering of those who had caught the sickness, sparing no details, in the hope that his graphic descriptions would cease the murmurings of descent. He told them of the fate of several villagers who had failed to join them within the confines of the manor house and its grounds and that several monks had died in pain.

"How do you know this?" someone asked.

"I saw Father Prior on the other side of the moat." Ruadhán must have thought quickly and Clémence admired him. "He shouted across and described what is happening."

Clémence knew the crowd would accept the news from one of the monks, especially one they knew and respected so well. She looked up at Ruadhán. She alone knew he had risked his well-being by venturing out on a mission of mercy for Agnes. He had seen for himself the full horror of the disease that was ravaging the population.

A cry from the road took her attention. "What have you done with the bridge, sir? Have you a raft, that we might come across?"

"We burned the crossing for our own protection."

"We need food for the road. That's all we ask. Not much. As you see, we are only six and one is dying from hunger. That is all it is. I tell you true, good knight. Let us in and you will see."

Ruadhán bent down and whispered in Clémence's ear. "We must plan our own protection. They only need to send a barrage of flaming arrows across the moat to cause havoc amongst the dwellings. Then they would be able to force an entry without too much difficulty during the chaos that might cause."

"We could soak the nearest cottages if we have enough time?" Clémence said.

"Yes, it might just help us, and if rains come tomorrow," he glanced up at the heavy, grey sky, "then we might avert danger this time. But we must be prepared for such an onslaught." Then he shouted to the visitors: "Camp there for the night and we shall do what we can tomorrow."

They all watched as the small company turned and moved away towards the woods and the village. It wasn't long before they heard distant shouting and calls. Were the men trying to force their way into the dwellings? Clémence doubted they would find much there, from what Ruadhán had said.

As night drew in, a glow appeared in the sky. "Look! I think they have fired a cottage," said a man. "Why would they do that?"

Ruadhán called his most trusted men, pointed to the glow in the night sky, explained his worries and the short-term plan. It wasn't long before the villagers formed a chain with leather buckets and drenched the small houses next to the moat. "Let us pray for rain," he said.

The next morning the small group returned.

Sir Ruadhán was ready for them. "Why did you set a fire? Was that some of our village?"

"You should have seen the rats, sir. There was no one there. Not alive, anyway," the leader of the group shouted. "We've saved you a task," he added, without heart or remorse. "Let us in, good sir. A small payment for our service in clearing that foul stench."

"We have nought to spare here," Ruadhán shouted back. "You best be on your way. We have no way to let you across, but we send our best wishes for good fortune."

"We cannot live on best wishes, friend."

"You were six, yesterday. Where is your companion?"

"He has gone to purgatory, for his sins must have been great."

"Had he the plague, then?"

"Maybe, maybe not. It is food we ask of you," the stranger said, turning the conversation. "Please, kind sir. We will not stay long enough to give you this pestilence."

"Be on your way. We have nothing for you here."

An hour passed. Ruadhán and several of the men kept watch. As suspected, they witnessed a flaming arrow arcing across the gloomy sky. It fell short of its mark but another followed, and another. This time the flames landed at the door of a dwelling, but the owner quenched it with half a bucket of water.

It was a half-hearted attack and no severe damage occurred, since the villagers had buckets of water ready and the attacker's had a limited supply of ammunition.

The breeze strengthened and droplets of rain quickly became a downpour. The villagers took the opportunity to fill their buckets with rainwater running from the roofs. The ruffian band turned away.

"Retain the watch," Ruadhán said, rain dripping from his hair onto already soaked shoulders. "We must be prepared for further attack, from them or from others passing this way. If one such band have heard of our situation, others may follow."

The attack shocked all those inside the moat and, though the band did not return. Everyone began to relax again. Life continued through the winter months, and most people were aware of their safety and grateful to Sir Ruadhán for his planning and support.

Clémence was privy to the fact that Ruadhán occasionally crossed the moat, but he always stayed away after each foray until he was certain that he carried no pestilence back with him. Despite this, the sights he saw were depressing, and Clémence began to wonder if the Great Mortality would ever pass.

Ruadhán had learned from Abbot Walter that over half the monks had become ill, and all but three had died in excruciating agony. It was a miracle that three that survived the disease, and none understood the reason. Ruadhán believed more strongly than ever that the illness was not due to God's wrath and punishment of sin, although prayers and services of thanks were profuse and their entreaties to God increased. One of those who recovered was Father Deodonatus. It made no sense that Father Deodonatus had survived when others, surely more worthy, had perished, despite what Abbot Walter said about prayer being their route to salvation.

The abbot encouraged the carrying of vials with liquid from distilled rose petals in them. "After all," the abbot had shouted to Ruadhán from a healthy distance, "roses are resistant to certain pests and so the liquid we have made should disinfect us and prevent us getting the plague. Our brother monks in Florence are practising this method."

Again, Ruadhán was unsure.

"There are many more rats these days," Abbot Walter shouted. "I wonder if we should burn the last of the empty houses and thus rid ourselves of these creatures. They climb the walls to nest in the thatch and multiply. Maybe they are carrying disease?"

"I think that's a sensible idea, Father. I shall leave it in your hands. Now I must go. I want to visit the church."

"Ah yes, our daughter. I have given her candles to burn, that she may ensure no rats penetrate her cell. Our brethren feed her bread and fish, and she has apples and ale. She is as well as expected and I hear her confession regularly. I know she prays much. God bless her piety and give her strength. I pray for her daily."

"Thank you, Father."

"God bless you, my son. You are performing God's work in keeping your people safe. May you receive what your heart desires." He made the sign of the cross over Ruadhán.

The two parted. As he walked towards the church, Ruadhán thought of what his heart most desired. Abbot Walter probably referred to keeping the community from harm, but his mind turned inexorably to Clémence. She avoided him with persistence, of that he was certain. In fairness, her work kept her occupied nearly all her waking hours, but when she wasn't working, she surrounded herself with people, teaching and reading, and even tried to make their lives enjoyable in these troubled times. She was popular, and her spirit and zest for life brought warmth in the cold winter months. The people were beginning to revere her.

He began to reason with himself and find an argument that would allow him a path forwards. King William I, the Great Conqueror, was of bastard birth, yet negotiated a marriage to Matilda, daughter of a count no less, and he rose to the highest rank in England. The great saint, Edward the Confessor, had promised William, albeit a distant cousin, the throne until Harold the Usurper had refused to give it to him. Clémence Masson was certainly no bastard. She was pure, wise, and beautiful. Why should he not take her for a wife? Then he remembered Lady Emma, to whom he was still foresworn. She was a pale comparison in all ways. And he didn't even know if she was still alive.

Thus his thoughts raced and before he realised it, he had reached the church.

Pushing open the door, he called out Agnes' name as he entered. He heard a scuffling.

A voice responded. "Go away, leave me alone. I do not want this constant pleading."

"It is only I, Ruadhán, to assure myself that you are well."

"Sir Ruadhán. Forgive me. I thought it was another."

"I shall not come close. It is not safe. The pestilence is still with us. I need to reassure your family that you are well."

"I am, sir."

Ruadhán paused. "Are you troubled by something, Agnes? Is it the cold? Or hunger? I can ask the monks..."

"No!" Her vehemence took him by surprise. Then she spoke more gently. "No, thank you. I am happy to be here."

"Agnes, I can tell, though I cannot see you, that you are troubled, please tell me."

He heard her sigh.

"All has been peaceful for many days. I know not exactly how long. In here I do not count the hours. But again, last night…" She trailed off.

"Last night?" he prompted.

"I can endure this physically. After all, is it not this chastisement of my reluctant body through which I shall gain immortality for my soul? It is the whispering and the terrible dreams that come unbidden in the dark. First there is the gentle tapping. It is soft, but it is there — tap, tap, tap. Then there is scrabbling at the door panel."

"Rats cannot get to you, Agnes, so long as you burn your candle."

"I am not afraid of rats, no. It is the words. They are so quiet, I am unsure if I've heard aright."

"What is said?" Ruadhán began to fear that she had lost her reason.

"It says, 'Let me in. Let me in, I beseech you.' I sing, I shout, I pray — anything to shut out the sound. Sometimes I see his eyes like burning coals at the grill in the dead of night. Just once, he said. 'No one need ever know.'"

"Who is this?" Ruadhán demanded. "Is it someone from the village?" He began to wonder if Daniel was still about. Clémence had told him that the young man had once hoped to marry Agnes. Food must have been almost non-existent for him, living rough in the woods and now it had been a long winter and there would have been even less. Rain and frost would be enough to kill a strong man — or send him mad. Perhaps his loneliness had become sinister.

Ruadhán shivered. Surely Daniel was long gone, or dead from the pestilence.

"Did you say it has been peaceful for a while, and now it has started again?"

"Yes, yes, exactly so." He heard a guttural cry. "I cannot bear it. I heard a hiss then a moaning and more scratching at the door If it returns night after night, I shall go mad."

He heard another sob. How would he relay this to Clémence? Perhaps he must gather some men, volunteers, and scour the woods for the fugitive. He could not allow this to continue.

"Fear not, Agnes. I promise I shall sort this problem for you. I'm going now, but I shall keep my vow to you. Keep faith, good sister."

"I shall, and thank you. Please tell my family, my sister, that I pray for their safety."

"And they do the same for you. God bless you."

Ruadhán left with a heavy heart. How could Agnes bear the cold, never mind the hunger and isolation. Was this all in her imagination? Outside, the wind swayed the bare branches of the trees, sending the clouds scudding across the flat, grey sky, and adding to his melancholy.

Ruadhán checked the stables to ensure all was well and then he visited the orchard. No work was going on except from one man finishing a repair to his roof. The knight nodded up at him. "Are you managing up there?" he shouted.

The man doffed his cap. "Yes, thank you, sir."

Since he could procrastinate no more, Ruadhán knew he must find Clémence and tell her what he had discovered with Agnes. With the decision made, he entered the warmth of the great hall. The fire blazed in the hearth and when he loudly proclaimed his arrival, someone came forward with ale for the lord of the manor. He took a deep draft before looking about and wondering where she might be. He looked in the kitchens where the heat was even greater and there was much activity.

The smell of rabbit stew assailed his nostrils and his stomach rumbled in response, but Clémence was not there.

"Where is Mistress Clémence?"

"Dunno, sir. Mayhap she went to visit her folk. She said she'd be back directly."

That was no good. Ruadhán did not want to impart his news in front of Merek and Catherine Masson. He and Clémmie would decide on a course of action before heaping further worries on her parents. Already her mother was weakening further and he had thought her not long for the world the last time he had witnessed her sunken, pallid cheeks.

When two children passed him, looking up at him and scuttling away, he realised he must stop frowning, since he probably looked fearsome. He turned to another group, standing to watch their game of Queek, charmed by their excitement as they shouted out which colour on the checkered board their stones would land. Eventually he asked, "Have you seen Mistress Masson?" They paused their game and pointed outside from whence he had arrived.

At last Ruadhán spied Clémence standing by the moat, where once the bridge had been. She gazed across the water and into the twilight. The sun had dipped below the horizon and the sky was a deepening hue of purple and black. A light breeze stirred her skirts. His heart was heavy and his footsteps sounded the same as he moved towards her. She looked over her shoulder and gave him a small smile. For several moments he said nothing, trying to work up the courage to tell her what he knew.

"We haven't spoken for a while," he finally ventured.

"No." Clémence shrugged, a gesture that he guessed belied her tension. "I've been busy."

"Indeed. I'm sorry if I said too much. Before, when I told you…"

"I remember what you said." There was a pause. "You are handfasted and I … I am a servant."

"In these strange days, the order of things is different." He was thinking of his musings as he walked to Edenham church and was about to tell her of King William I when she spoke.

"Well, we'll have to see if that's true when this pestilence passes, as it surely must. Things may return to the old order and we must still be distanced from each other, as we were before. And Lady Emma may yet return."

Ruadhán sighed. "I have other news, regarding your sister Agnes."

"Is she ill?" Clémence turned to face him, fear in her eyes.

"She is well. She has as many candles as she needs and the monks look after her well. But she is frightened."

"Frightened? Of what? Surely the pestilence cannot claim her. She is isolated and alone."

Ruadhán took a deep breath. "Someone is scrabbling at her door each night and begging to be let within her cell."

Clémence gasped and her hand flew to her mouth.

"She is safe, but it is unsettling her. She said there was a respite for some days, but then it started again, a soft tap-tapping and then pleading. I fear that if it continues, it will drive her mad."

"Who would do this?"

"I wondered if it was Daniel Farmer. Who else could it be? I understand he said that he would stay around for a while in the woods to watch out for Agnes. Perhaps their separation has driven *him* insane."

Clémence put her hand to her forehead and some of her hair escaped from her kerchief. "I cannot believe that of Daniel. He wanted to marry my sister — he revered her. He would not stoop to such cruelty, surely?" She shivered.

"Come, let us move from here. It's cold now the daylight has gone. Tomorrow, I shall ask two volunteers to cross the moat with me and help me to scour the woods."

"Surely Daniel could not survive this long, living rough like that?"

"It would be possible. He could gather berries and snare rabbits. There will have been grain in the fields and beans around the houses which he might have gathered before they rotted."

"But the plague…" Clémence trailed off and shook her head. "He surely will be far away by now, for his own safety and protection."

"I don't know, perhaps you are correct, but I must help Agnes back to a peaceful existence. I promised her."

Clémence thanked him before she turned to enter the great hall and help with the mealtime preparation.

Ruadhán watched her go, watching as she tucked the strands of autumn-coloured curls under kerchief, as he so longed to do.

Late that night, while the others slept, Clémence cracked the shutters as she had grown accustomed to do. Several women shared the room and without fresh air, she worried about normal winter diseases spreading, never mind the pestilence that may well thrive on fetid air, for all she knew. She made a mental inventory of the herbs and spices they had left in store. Henbane and hemlock were still in profusion for aching joints; there was limited coriander for a fever; wormwood, mint and balm for stomach pains and sickness were still plentiful; the supply of myrrh was extremely limited; there was plenty of vinegar for wounds, of course. As she stood by the opening, absorbing the gentle sounds of the night, a movement caught her eye.

The clouds parted and the bright moon shone down, silvering the fields, removing all the aura of disuse and neglect, and falsely endowing beauty and Clémence peered across the land. She discerned a figure swathed in a cloak, the hood pulled well-down over their face. A cold prickle of fear ran down her spine and she prepared to shout a warning, aware that the watch had become lax after so long without attack or even any approach by strangers.

As the figure approached, they lowered their hood and Clémence gasped. It was Daniel. She would know him anywhere. After all, they had played together as children, lived closely. She had known him all her life. Was it he who had been such a scourge to Agnes? Surely not. But if not him, then who?

She could not call across to him. Everyone in the bedchamber would hear her and the hall was full of sleeping bodies at this hour, so she could not go downstairs. She waved to gain his attention. As she watched and waited, Daniel's coarse whisper reached her. "I shall save her. Fear not." Then he turned and ran towards the woods, his shadow disappearing among the trees.

"Who goes there?" The watch had awoken. "Show yourself. We have arms." The guard must have thought he imagined it as all had returned to hushed tranquillity.

Clémence returned to her bed, her thoughts racing. She did not believe that Daniel was torturing her sister. But if not he, then who, and how could he save her?

CHAPTER 17

Ruadhán had a problem to solve and a decision to make. How could he leave the compound to search the woods without the manor house workers and village people hearing of his foray? He would need two trusted companions to accompany him. If everyone knew he had been across the moat before, and was planning to go again, what would stop many thinking it was safe for them to do so, too? Perhaps the worst of the pestilence had passed, but he did not know and was unwilling to take that risk. All those inside the moat had so far survived, but he knew from his conversations with Abbot Walter that many of the monks at Vaudey Abbey had perished, no doubt because they continued to minister to those who had refused to leave their land and join him in the manor grounds.

It was a risk he must take. If he chose his companions wisely and swore them to secrecy, perhaps he might accomplish the task with success. He also had a plan to burn the derelict cottages, to rid the land of as many rats and as much filth as possible. The villagers could rebuild with relative speed if they survived this Great Mortality.

One person he would ask to volunteer would be the messenger, Joseph Mercer. Who might he choose for the other? He considered Merek Masson, but his family needed him. He thought hard. Perhaps the two of them would suffice. The wooded areas were large, but Daniel would not be far away, surely. Three would be better. They could fan out and cover the distances in much less time. He had a sudden idea, but decided he must speak to Clémence first. He welcomed her good counsel.

"I have a notion but would like your opinion of it," Ruadhán said. He and Clémence were in the gardens. Few were about since it was so cold. Their feet left imprints in the frosted grass, soaking Clémence's slippers, but she said nothing.

"Is it concerning the search you spoke of last eve?" she asked.

"Yes. I will ask Joseph Mercer to accompany me."

"That's a good idea. He has no family, so no one to look after, and none to tell tales. Will you ask anyone else?"

"This is the problem. I wondered if your father should come," he said, before hurrying on. "But I am sure that your family need him."

Ruadhán risked a glance and could see that Clémence was giving his suggestion serious contemplation.

"It would be better if you took Mattie, than my father. He is a man now. Father is too involved with Agnes' situation and anyway, Mother needs him more than ever. If Father went, Mattie would not be able to hold his thoughts if asked."

Ruadhán was silent while he considered her idea. "I am certain we will be safe from the pestilence. I have been outside twice already and I have the methods we must use to remain so. I'll speak with your father. The other thing I propose is to fire the unused cottages. By now, that may well be all of them." He sighed. "It will kill all the rats and ensure they have no places to nest. If we all work together when this disease is done, then we will rebuild with great speed."

Clémence nodded. "I detest those creatures and am not convinced of other reasons for the disease, put forward by the church, that it is God's punishment. Surely, cleanliness takes us closer to safety. I'm certain that's the best idea." She touched his arm lightly. "Godspeed, Ruadhán."

On reaching the Masson's dwelling, Ruadhán knocked and asked for a private word with Merek. As they walked parallel with the moat, he described what Agnes had told him and what he proposed to do about it.

Merek looked shocked, but he agreed. "I find it hard to accept that Daniel Farmer would do such a thing. Mattie is a young man and craves a man's responsibilities. I will not tell Catherine, though. I shall simply say you have a special task for him which may take several days."

Ruadhán placed a hand on the older man's shoulder. "Thank you, Merek. I know I can rely on your loyalty."

"'Tis I who must thank you, sir, for what you are proposing for my daughter's safety and well-being."

It was exceedingly early the following morning, just after Matins, when the only people who were moving about would be the monks at Vaudey Abbey making their sleepy return to their beds. Daylight at this time of year was still four hours away. The three men retrieved the old raft hidden in the undergrowth. From time to time, and by his own hand, Ruadhán had maintained it, once replacing a rotten plank, and ensuring it would carry him over the waters of the moat. The three companions certainly wouldn't want to fall into the water. It was bitterly cold with a few stars in the sky, the grass bejewelled with frost.

The traverse was easy, as it turned out, and they hurried across the fields, keeping low, towards the woods. The plan was to spread out and cover as much space as possible in a brief time.

"If you see anything, blow on a grass blade to alert the other two," Ruadhán said. "The sound will travel well enough."

"You mean like this?" Mattie picked a coarse blade and stretched it vertically between his thumbs. "I used to practise this as a boy." He was about to demonstrate when Ruadhán closed his own hand over the young man's.

"Not yet," he whispered. "We don't wish to alert anyone to our presence. Pretend you are stalking deer or a wild boar. You must be silent, stealthy, so you do not alert the prey. Only make the call if you need us to come."

Mattie nodded.

"We will meet back here at Sext. The sun, if it comes, will be high and we shall rest and eat before looking again the other way."

They set off and after a few paces Ruadhán stopped to listen, gratified that Mattie, and indeed Joseph, had taken him at his word and were moving in silence.

They all knew the formation of trees well, having played in these woods as children and hunted as grown men. Ruadhán's eyes had adjusted to the dark, but he found nothing of note. There was no warning sound from the others. At one point something large scuttled away, probably a badger from the noisy, snorting sound it made. There were the usual creaks of tree limbs, and some bird, startled, flew away, but that was all. He walked the paths slowly, some made by people and some by animals. In the distance he heard the bells for Prime. It would be daylight in about an hour. He stopped, pushed his cloak back over one shoulder, and took the leather bottle which hung from his belt. Taking a deep gulp, he quaffed the liquid to slake his thirst. The weak ale did its job and he moved on.

He hadn't gone far before a shriek rent the air. Ruadhán immediately thought of a fox, but it was the wrong time of year. Then there was a howl and an unearthly bellow. He began to run.

As he tore through the forest, Ruadhán ignored the brambles that tore at his clothes. At one point he stumbled over a fallen log buried in the undergrowth, but swiftly regained his footing. Just then, he heard their agreed sound. A deep warble from a vibrating blade of grass between someone's thumbs, not unlike the call of a male tawny owl. He altered course as he heard it again, and as he did so, he also heard the sound of someone else running. The sound emanated from somewhere much closer and very soon he came upon a scene he would never forget.

Clémence watched from the shadows of the manor house wall, wrapped in her cloak. She had kept vigil for several nights, awaiting Ruadhán's return. On his previous forays, he had stayed away long enough to prove that no disease was returning with him to their compound. He could come at any time now — if he was coming at all. Clémence shivered and held her arms tighter around her body. The cold seeped in deceitfully, taking all sensation. Suddenly, she thought she heard shuffling on the far side of the moat. Yes. Several figures emerged from the darkness. Three people. Her heart started pounding. It was them!

Together they pulled the raft from its hiding place among the rough scrub beside a hedge and lowered it gingerly into the water. Every sound reverberated in the stillness of the night. As the small company neared, Clémence showed herself and whispered a welcome. She was so relieved to see Ruadhan, Mattie and Joseph, now returned, and appearing in good health. After they stowed the raft back in its hiding place, Mattie approached and hugged her.

She held him from her then, and said, "Are you well, and in one piece?"

"Yes, we are all in good shape but we saw —"

"Let's get inside, lad, before we all freeze," Ruadhan interrupted. "Time to tell our story soon enough."

Clémence went to the kitchen and prepared three mugs of mulled wine for the men. They followed her. As she added the spices — cinnamon, cloves, and even the new and precious sugar, she was grateful to Joan who had acquired them from a travelling merchant, who in turn had bought them in the seaport of Boston. The pungent aroma was uplifting. They sat on stools at the workbench, knowing no one would disturb them since all those in the great hall slept. It was cosy among the shadows and the lingering smells of food, with the heat of the great fires used for cooking. Clémence could wait no longer. "Well?" she asked.

"We found him. It was shocking," Mattie said in a rush. Clémence turned a questioning look at Ruadhán.

"The lad is correct," he said, "it was indeed shocking. There was nought we could do for him."

"Who? Daniel?"

Ruadhán shook his head. "I am not making myself plain. We are all so weary. I'll start again. It was Father Deodonatus."

Clémence gasped. "What happened?"

"We had separated when I heard a terrible cry. I ran through the woods with all speed, fearing for young Mattie, or Joseph." He acknowledged his companion with a nod. "When I arrived at the scene, Father Deodonatus was lying, slain. It was an awful sight. He had been stabbed, the knife still within him, close to his heart. He had many cuts, as if attacked in a frenzy, and his throat was slit from ear to ear."

Clémence was stunned. "Who would do such a thing, and why? But what of Daniel and my sister, Agnes?"

"Sir Ruadhán went to visit your sister alone, Mistress Clémence," said Joseph. "We didn't want her to be frightened with so many approaching her at night."

Clémence could contain her impatience no longer. "What did she say? Is she all right? Did she name Daniel as her aggressor?"

"No, she did not," said Ruadhán. "She was clear. It was not Daniel. He has never been anything but kind."

Clémence waited, tension pulsing through her whole body.

"It was Father Deodonatus. It was he who was pleading to be let into her cell. And now he has paid the price for his sins, and we may never know who is responsible."

"Perhaps it was Daniel," whispered Clémence.

"Yes, I think perhaps it may have been, and may God have mercy on him for the act."

Joseph stood and announced he was off to find his pallet and sleep for what little was left of the night. Mattie stood, kissed his sister's cheek and then, he too, bade farewell.

Clémence stood and hugged him. "Thank you, brother. You have been wonderful and good and our whole family will remember your bravery." He nodded in manly fashion but his face glowed in the warmth of her words.

She turned to Ruadhán. "I cannot blame Daniel, if indeed it were he. And I cannot thank you enough. What have you done with Father Deodonatus' body?"

"We buried him deep in the woods. None will find him. The brothers at the monastery will think he has either succumbed to the plague or run off. I'm certain there will be no further enquiry."

Clémence could contain her tears no longer. The relief that her sister was safe, those she loved so dearly were well, and her long hours of vigil were over, was too much.

Ruadhan rose, came around the bench, and took a stool next to her. After a moment his arm came round her shoulder and she leaned into him and wept. He whispered into her hair gently, as if comforting a child. She knew not what he said but it didn't matter. The warmth of his body was enough.

The bells for Lauds chimed. "It will soon be light," Clémence said. "I cannot thank you enough." She sat up and wiped her eyes. Suddenly exhausted, when she looked into Ruadhán's eyes, she saw that he was too. She leaned forward and kissed the side of his face.

Ruadhán smiled. His kindness and love shone out and wrapped her in its warmth.

Ruadhán gathered the whole company together. For the first time, he was nervous about the decision he had taken. When the villagers had first arrived at his door, they had been frightened of the forthcoming pestilence and worried about what would happen. Each person had voiced their gratitude for his hospitality. Now, thrust into close confinement for a long period of time, people were restless.

They would have seen the glow of the fires and smelt the burning wood and thatch. Flakes of charred material flew in the breeze, but the strong, sweet odour of burning flesh was the most alarming of all.

"I went on a mission with two others. It was essential." A stunned silence greeted this announcement, but was soon replaced by puzzled mutterings. Ruadhán raised his voice. "I had to ensure the safety of Agnes Masson. She was in mortal danger, but all is well now. She may continue to live in peace."

"What about our houses?" a voice called out.

"And our possessions?" shouted another.

Ruadhán took a deep breath. Angry faces looked up at him. Serfs and workers they might be, and he, their lord and master, but he was aware they had suffered severe privations over the last months.

"You are right to ask. I have seen our friends and neighbours, people we have known, lying dead from this plague, having suffered most horribly. I wish they had joined us here." He paused to clear his throat. "The rats, which have multiplied unbelievably, were living in those houses, and in yours, with a freedom to feed on … well … whatever they could find. I can say no more. The sights and smells will stay with me for an exceedingly long time."

There was restlessness and people looked down at their shuffling feet or across to the side walls of the hall, anywhere but at their master in his distress and took in the horror of what he said.

"When I saw the vermin, I decided the only way to deal with it was to set fire to everything. I shall compensate you. We shall all help each other to rebuild and I shall ensure the materials are available, free of cost. Your possessions, I can do nothing about." He played for time to prevent his eyes filling with tears, spreading his arms in a gesture of helplessness. "When you came here, I said to bring your most valued treasures. I'm sorry."

Clémence should not have been surprised but it still came as a shock when Sir Aedric appeared in the distance, approaching the manor with three companions.

"I would recognise his courser anywhere," Ruadhán said as he stood beside her near the moat, gazing across. Several other people gathered around as they heard the beating of hooves.

"Surely, he'll be allowed to come across," one man in the crowd said.

"Why should he? He hasn't been near in all these months," another answered.

"He was our lord when Sir Ruadhán was away. He was happy enough to have his uncle's help then," someone muttered. It was Marie, always around to stir trouble.

Clémence turned and answered. "Sir Ruadhán had no choice but to go and serve his king, and I don't remember Sir Aedric making such a good fist of things. You have a short memory, Marie Miller, if you have forgotten he spent all his time drinking while the land did not prosper well. I've a mind he only comes now because he wants something for himself."

"You haven't fared so ill yourself in recent months, Mistress Clémence," Marie said.

"And neither have you. If Sir Ruadhán had not taken us in, we would all be dead, and in a most ugly manner."

Marie shrugged but said no more as several around her nodded their agreement with Clémence.

Meanwhile, the horsemen had neared the moat. Sir Aedric had increased in girth over the many months of absence and he did not look well for that. His hair was long and his beard was ragged. His companions looked no better. They had been on the road, of course, but their faces had an unhealthy pallor.

"Where is the bridge?" Aedric shouted across. "How are we supposed to come across and take refuge?"

"We burned it many months ago," Ruadhán shouted back. "We are in confinement here but safe as a result. Have you ridden far?"

"From my own manor, of course. Come along, now. We are tired from our travels and have a deep hunger. We need ale, too."

Clémence was desperate to know if Lady Emma followed in a carriage or a cart, but she could not shout across as Ruadhán had done.

"Where are the other men who left with you? You are a small company, now."

Aedric chose to ignore the question and instead responded with, "All the easier for you to let us come across, Nephew. We shall not drain your resources with our number. I have heard that you all live well here, that you have food a plenty."

"Only because our lord and master, and Mistress Clémence, are wise and thrifty and have planned well," someone from the crowd took the courage to shout out.

"Ah! Mistress Clémence. So that's how it lies, is it? She always was one with her eyes on a bigger prize."

"You will say no more, Uncle. We cannot let you cross. We are not allowing anyone, and it has kept us healthy all these months. Where is my Lady Emma? Is she safe and well?"

Aedric hawked and spat the contents of his throat. "Yes, well… She's dead and probably just as well. It was twins, so she must have lain with two men who impregnated her at the same time. Where is the sanctity in that?"

Clémence gasped. She recognised the lie for what it was. There was little doubt in her mind that Aedric had taken advantage of Emma's innocence, as he had with Hawise. She said a silent prayer for both young women. He had set his eyes on Lady Emma as a means of overtaking Ruadhán's plans. It was another means of retaliating for the perceived wrong his own brother had done him by leaving his property to his young son.

"Girls, the babies would have been, too. Nothing to do with me, of course. I know I can provide lusty boys." He laughed uproariously and looked at his companions, who grinned at him. "She had her sights on me, of course, but that was a long time ago. Before all this trouble." His voice took on a whining tone. "Now let us in, Nephew."

"You may make camp there and I shall arrange for food to be sent to you. We will float something across on a plank. The weather is set fair, but you shall approach no further." Ruadhán turned away with resolution.

Clémence watched him stride away and the crowd dissipated. The excitement was over. Most were mumbling in agreement with their lord, and she gleaned that Aedric was unpopular, his presence not wanted. The small group across the moat huddled together in deep conversation. It was some hours later when next she looked. It was a shock.

One of the men accompanying Aedric lay on the far bank of the moat. He called in a feeble voice when he saw her, lifting his arm for succour. She turned and ran to the hall to relay what she had seen. Upon her return with Ruadhán, a small number of villagers had gathered, having finished their work for the day.

"God and all his saints preserve us from that," said one. "It is sent from the Devil himself, most surely."

It was a shocking sight. The man had ripped away his clothing in his distress, revealing his sores and buboes to the sky and the watching villagers. He appeared to be unconscious or dead even. Ruadhán made the sign of the cross and several of the villagers fell to their knees in prayer. Old Father Pious from the abbey, who tended them all these months, arrived and began prayers for the dead and dying.

Of Aedric and the other two men there was no sign.

Upon her return to the hall, Clémence saw Ruadhán standing by the fireplace, deep in thought. He spoke without looking at her. "I have condemned my uncle to a terrible death."

Clémence knew that since Aedric had been in the company of that poor fellow for many days, his life was almost certainly at risk.

"Yes, but you saved a whole community. And you must know it was Aedric who was responsible for the death of Hawise and, I believe, of Lady Emma."

Ruadhán sighed heavily and nodded. "I do. And now there are rumours of war re-starting with the French. The Scots are collecting in the north, too. Will we never be free to live here with contentment and joy?"

A chill stole down Clémence's spine. "Surely not again, and so soon after all the privations? How have you heard of this here in our confinement?"

"From Father Prior, when I was away with Joseph and Mattie."

"I see." Clémence paused. "The lull in the fighting during this time of fearful pestilence has been a godsend. Surely there will be double the risk to leave and join a military force so soon."

"We shall see. At the moment it is just rumour, but he has heard that the plague is leaving our region, although it is still troubling the north and Scotland is suffering severely."

"So, you may be going to France again?" Clémence was devastated at the news.

"My lord the Duke of Lancaster is preparing on the coast and I owe him allegiance through Baron de Beaumont, child that he is."

"Oh!" Clémence lowered her eyes.

"Will you miss me? If, of course, it comes to aught."

She glanced up and saw his smile, mischievous in the fire's glow. "I think you know the answer." She spoke quietly and in earnest.

"I am no longer handfast, it would seem."

"No."

"I recalled, some time ago, that even our king who became William I was born out of wedlock, and while you are not in that group, being lower born is no barrier. I would make you my wife in an instant, if you would consent."

"Oh? And what would your serfs and even the sokemen say to that? That I have risen above my station and am no better than I should be. That's what."

"Clémmie. Please consider what I ask. It is with my heart. I have loved you for so long. I desire no other, and birth or status is nothing to me."

"Easy for you to say, sir, from the height of your given rights. I would be happy, indeed." She paused to fight back the revealing tears. "But I would also need the respect of those around me." The recent words of Sir Aedric echoed through her mind. *Mistress Clémence. So that's how it lies, is it? She always was one with her eyes on a bigger prize.*

CHAPTER 18

There was optimism in the air. Spring turned to early summer but trees still wore their vibrant green. Alder, birch, and willow, which fared so opulently on the rich fen soil, were in full leaf. Bluebells were giving way to foxgloves, which were happy to sprout anywhere but relished the shade afforded by the foliage above. Bluetits darted from one branch to another, while doves, thrushes, and robins sang with joy. Perhaps they, too, knew the plague was passing. Clémence stood for a moment and closed her eyes to breathe in the sweet-smelling fragrances enveloping her. When she opened them again, it was to see Ruadhán waiting for her to catch up. She danced towards him, grinning at the pleasures of being free at last, and with the man she loved. Even if she could not give herself to him, she was enjoying this freedom. He took her hand and together they trod the path that was quite overgrown with absence of use over the last twenty-two months.

"I can hardly believe we have been confined for so long," she said. "It has seemed an age and yet it has passed quickly enough. It's a strange thing, the measurement of time."

Ruadhán leaned down and kissed her lips as her face lifted to his. Their lips met again. This time with deeper enthusiasm. Clémence wanted to lie with him. Now that Lady Emma was no longer going to claim him, she was prepared to throw all restraint to the heavens — until a small worm of caution held her back. She thought of Hawise.

Then he pulled away. "Much as I would prefer to kiss you, we're here to mark the trees for felling. If we are to replace the bridge we burned all those months ago, we must make haste. Joseph and the others will catch us up at any moment."

"There is a cluster of oaks over that way." Clémence nodded in the direction of the trees. "They would be tall and strong enough for the main struts, wouldn't they?"

"Indeed. Let's go and mark the straightest and most sturdy and then head back to the manor. The others will cut it and haul it back with the horses."

"That was quite a task, getting the coursers across the moat and up the bank. I wondered if they were going to flounder. I was becoming quite worried for them."

"They are powerful beasts. The ponies certainly would not have had the strength. Even the coursers are unaccustomed to such demanding work and will need exercising so they are battle ready, should we get the call."

The smile left Clémence's face. "Is that likely?"

"I fear it is. King Edward has been preparing the Cinque Ports and demanding that the merchants' cogs be made ready. He fears the French are on the move again, now the pestilence is retreating. I hear men will be pressed, in the ports and the surrounding countryside, if crews are insufficient. Carlos de la Cerda's fleet has been preying on English ships since Edward and his son returned after defeating the attempt of the French to regain Calais. They held it for the English, praise God."

"I thought there was a truce between our countries? Surely the French have suffered just as we with this Great Mortality?"

"It is true, but a breach of the truce was made when the French killed the captain of the Gascon wine fleet heading for our south coast. De la Cerda had the sailors thrown overboard, too. Now, Edward has appointed Lord Morley to Admiral of the Northern Fleet and the king has headed south again, swearing to take full command. The duke of Lancaster is to join the force and I shall have to go, as his man."

"But what about our lands here? There is so much to organise and repair. The people will need guidance for the rebuilding of their houses. The fields are dormant and we have missed the spring planting. We are fewer in number since those who would not join us have perished. There are only half the monks that there were. The people need your leadership."

"And they will have it while I am here and you shall help me. The first thing to do is rebuild the bridge, so we may come and go with ease again. The serfs and workers will be scared to leave, I fear. I need to you to be a leader, too."

"Me?"

"Yes." Ruadhán stopped walking and turned to face her. "Have you not been running the household for many months now? Have you not made a success of planning and using the resources that could so easily have run dry? You have encouraged, cajoled, and insisted when things were difficult. You have ensured everyone is busy, and in so doing you have developed a valuable community. Surely you have not forgotten the rumble of insurrection when Aedric reappeared. Clémmie, my love, you can do this, even if I must leave for a while.

"I shall speak to the people," he said. "I shall tell them of my instructions. Joseph will be there to help you. I shall not take him with me. The community respect you. They will listen. It will not be the first time a woman has stepped into the breach. Think back to the mother of King Richard, the one they call the Lionheart. She was fierce and brave."

"Queen Eleanor was certainly indomitable. I don't think I wish to be as ferocious as she." Clémence chortled at the thought.

"Perhaps not, but you will manage our small community, and do it well." Ruadhán drew her into his arms and she rested her cheek on his jerkin. All she wanted was to stay like this, to forget the world with its troubles. She needed him to stay and rebuild the village. What did she know of all this? Then she stood upright. She would do whatever was necessary. Joseph Mercer would stand by her and her father was there for advice.

The clink of harness and chains broke the spell and two men appeared, leading horses. Their brown work boots resounded on the beaten earth, as did the horses hooves. The horses would pull the tree trunk through the woods towards the manor, where the men would set to with saws, axes, and eventually planing blades to make the main beams and struts for a new bridge. They would joint and peg it to ensure it was sturdy enough to take the heavy traffic demanded of it. There was an urgency. If their liege called his lordship to action soon, horses and wagons, heavily laden, would need access to the outside world.

Ruadhán hailed his workers and together they all stepped forward to identify the trees to be felled.

Clémence rowed across the moat and hurried to her parents' dwelling. If she was to manage the manor household in Ruadhán's absence, then she wanted to share this news with them and discuss the rebuilding programme that would start soon. Suddenly she was bursting with ideas and enthusiasm. It was not a position to which she had been born, but it was one that, during the pestilence, seemed to have worked well for the good of all. Although confinement was easing, many of the villagers were still nervous about leaving the compound. They feared the Great Mortality might still be lurking, although fields needed reclaiming from the couch grass and other weeds which had seeded themselves.

Bounding through the door, she found the living area empty. Thinking that her father, and perhaps even her mother, might be tending their small vegetable plot, she looked there. No one. Perhaps they were taking a stroll around the orchard. As she turned, her father appeared. His expression was one of concern. Clémence hurried towards him.

"Father, what is it?"

"It's your mother."

"What has happened?" Clémence did not wait for an answer as she rushed around to the door again. Clutching her skirts, she hurried up the ladder to the sleeping area above. Catherine knelt beside Arthur's small body, her shoulders heaving.

Clémence flung herself down and held her mothers' bony shoulders. "But … but when I was last here, Arthur was toddling about downstairs. I know he's never been strong, and was coughing, but he's been doing that since he was a babe… I don't understand. Oh, Mother!"

Anger engulfed her. They had survived the awful pestilence and now this. It was so unfair. Shivering tears coursed down Catherine's pale cheeks. A gulp and a strangled howl burst forth and great racking sobs overtook her. As they knelt together, tears flowed from Clémence's eyes, as much for her mother as for her tiny brother. They stayed like that for some time until she heard Catherine croak, "Leave me for a while."

With reluctance Clémence climbed back down to find her father sitting in the chair, his head in his hands. She crouched beside him and placed a hand on his shoulder. "What happened, Father?"

Merek took a deep, shuddering breath. "We found him with a great handful of bread — half the loaf was gone. He found it on the side over there —" he nodded to the board — "and simply ate his fill. You know how it's always disagreed with him."

Clémence nodded and waited for him to continue. "His throat swelled almost straight away and he had trouble breathing. He ... he turned blue." Tears ran down Merek's cheeks. "I picked him up, but by the time I had carried him up the steps, he had passed away." He dashed a hand across his eyes. "Your mother thinks it's her fault because the bread was left within his reach." He shrugged in hopeless resignation.

Clémence took a deep breath. "Sir Ruadhán will have him buried in the graveyard of the manor house, and then you may visit easily. It's nobody's fault. Arthur was never strong."

Merek cleared his throat and stood. "I must return to your mother."

Clémence nodded. "I'll return soon."

Merek paused. "Why did you come? Did you need something?"

"It will keep." She watched as he disappeared into the loft area. *How will Mother cope with this? She is so weak already. I must visit each day and bring some broth to give her strength.*

Most of the villagers turned out for the internment, but despite the sunshine and bird song, the funeral was a solemn affair.

Clémence did as she had promised, but over the next week Catherine barely ate. She seemed not to be able to see beyond each bleak day, and in her grief she retreated into herself. They knew they were losing her.

The day that arrived seemed inevitable, and Catherine's grave lay next to her small son, leaving Merek to grieve all over again.

Clémence lost herself in her work around the manor, falling exhausted into bed each night. She visited Merek and ensured he and Mattie ate sufficient. She knew she must visit Agnes in

189

her enclave, now that greater freedom was allowed, but she procrastinated. She was cross with Agnes for retreating, when perhaps she could have helped.

Ruadhán supervised the building of the new bridge and watched Clémence with concern. Each day the structure grew and it wasn't long before it was complete. Then the news arrived that he had feared. He would have to return to battle. Gone was the latent excitement, the enthusiasm for combat, and thoughts of glory. All he wanted was to remain at the manor, rebuild the village for his people, and, most of all, to comfort Clémence in any way she would allow.

He would have to speak with her and formulate a plan for them all. Perhaps it might help the malaise which enveloped her.

Ruadhán's opportunity to speak with Clémence came when she brought a pot of rich gruel and some bread out to the men as they finished their work on the bridge. He was standing directing the last of it. After she had placed the food on the trestle and called the men, she turned to leave. He fell into step beside her.

"I would speak with you. It's important. Perhaps we might go to the gardens, where it will be quieter at this time."

"Certainly, if you wish it," she replied, but there was no joy or enthusiasm. That had disappeared the day they laid Catherine to rest.

He led her to a secluded area away from dwellings where women might be sitting outside spinning or weaving, children crawling in the sun, young girls tending the cooking pots. The men had returned to their fields or to the mill, the forge, or other such trades.

They stood in the shade of an ash tree and Clémence leaned her back against the trunk.

"The Castilian fleet employed by the French are no more than pirates, preying on English shipping, despite the truce between England and France," he said. "It sounds like another battle with the French is looming.

"Carlos de la Cerda ordered the pillaging of ships sailing for England from Bordeaux. He organised ransacking and rape at Portsmouth, Southampton, and along the coast to Dungeness, and now it has come to a head. King Edward has had enough.

"The king and the Black Prince are heading to the coast. Even his third son, John of Gaunt, is going, and he's only eleven. The truce King Edward signed with the French is over. It never really took place." He pressed home his point. "The Beaumonts at Folkingham are the Duke of Lancaster's men, as am I."

"I know where allegiances lie." Clémence sighed. "You cannot gainsay the most powerful of Edwards's advisers."

"Know this, though, my dear," Ruadhán looked into her downcast face, "this time I have no desire to go. I would stay here and mend my community. But go I must. I have no choice."

She looked up into his eyes. "I know."

"You must manage in my place, and with the help of others the re-building here will continue. Isn't this what you've always wanted — to do what men do, to have a position of responsibility and to achieve as an equal?"

He recognised a glint in her gaze as she looked up at him.

"I see I have revived some self-knowledge in you. Think back over the years when you railed against your lot."

"I will, and when you return you will see of what I am capable."

"I believe I already know." Ruadhán grinned. He would leave with a heavy heart, but at least he could be confident that the demesne would be safe in her hands. Before they walked back to the manor, he plucked a flower and presented it to her.

At last she smiled. "Thank you. I shall place it between linen in my box of treasures."

Ruadhán and his retinue where prepared, mounted and gone all too soon. Clémence was determined to make progress and counsel her leading sokemen. She had called them together into the small parlour. Seated in a circle, there was no obvious hierarchy, but it was clear to all who led the meeting.

"I am convinced the main cause of the Great Mortality was filth and an unhealthy accumulation of rats. They live in thatch and under floors. They climb inside walls and breed in areas of excrement. Our new buildings in the village must reduce this possibility."

The men around her nodded. "I believe you are correct, my lady," said Joseph Mercer.

"I am not your lady, but thank you for the compliment. I am still Mistress Clémence. No more. I am most gratified that Sir Ruadhán trusts me in his absence."

"As do we, my lady."

Clémence ignored the title he bestowed this time, but noted the nods around the room. "The rats seem to have stayed away from the roofs that we made from planking. Perhaps we might line the new properties with that before we put thatch over the top. It will be more costly. What do you think?"

"Aye, but it will make the houses warmer."

"We must designate a place for slops well away from dwellings." As Clémence spoke, she was determined this would be a key feature of the new village. "The trough that we constructed before works well. I suggest that we build similar for each dwelling so that effluent runs away into a deep pit away from each cott."

The meeting continued, with each man encouraged to give his opinion. Clémence relied on their support, both with ideas and with chivvying the men of the community to give extra time to the rebuilding after their work in the fields. There would be some who dissented, so it was up to her to convince them that the community would be healthier as a result. Ruadhán had already said he would pay for the materials, but she must remind them of this and point out the advantages. One or two had become content with the easy life they had been leading within the moat. However, food was becoming scarcer now, and it was vital they resume the old life.

"Please call a gathering of all the workers, not just the sokemen and upper serfs. This is something that involves us all." She was aware that the way she presented the plans was key.

Clémence prayed that morning for wisdom and strength. When the time came, she asked questions of the community for which she gave immediate answers. She was persuasive but spoke with passion and authenticity, reminding them all of what Ruadhán had done to ensure their safety.

Only one spoke out, and it was no surprise to Clémence that it was Marie. Those around her shouted her down, and the moment passed. Clémence had no doubt anymore that Marie would always be an irritant, but she had no power to stir real trouble.

After everyone had dispersed to their daily tasks, Clémence took a deep breath before she searched for refreshment and continued with her day. Those she had identified to cut wood, make wattle, prepare the daub, and fashion water conduits were set to work for as long as daylight permitted, such was the enthusiasm she had engendered.

On the morrow, she would visit Abbot Walter at Grimsthorpe monastery and ask for his help with the elderly who had no family. The hospitaller would need to be engaged to administer until they were all settled into their new accommodation. She was grateful that all the monks were devoted and kind. Only one had been the bad apple. And now he was gone. Her thoughts turned to Agnes, and Clémence felt a small stab of guilt that she had not visited her sister more often.

At the end of each day, she opened her chest of treasures and looked at all the things inside which brought so many cherished memories. Things which might be little to another but which were the map of her life brought Ruadhán closer. Clémence wondered how he was faring before sleep claimed her. She worried for him and not knowing where he was, or with what he had to contend, was difficult. Despite being proud of her own achievements, she would have preferred to share them with him. Her prayers before slumber were all for him and she was desperately sorry that she had been reticent during the days before he left. She had been so consumed by grief for her mother and her brother. Now that Ruadhán was gone from the manor, it was imperative she stay strong. She would go to see her sister, confide in her, and ask for her prayers.

CHAPTER 19

There was preparation for war on both sides of the English Channel and Ruadhán was nervous. This was not to be a situation with which he was familiar.

"It won't be so very different to a land battle once we've sent over the grappling hooks," one man said. "All the ships will end up tied together and we'll take arms in the normal way. There may be some ramming before that, but our cogs have sharp bows. The Castilian carracks may be larger but we're manoeuvrable."

Ruadhán wondered which ship the Duke of Lancaster would command, but perhaps as a lesser knight he would himself be placed with Lord Stafford, Lord Percy, Earl Arundel or any one of the other redoubtable lords of the realm. He knew that King Edward favoured *Cog Thomas* and would have his younger son with him. He'd heard the Black Prince would command another cog. As it transpired, Ruadhán was on the *Michael*, which seemed appropriate as the church at Edenham had that connection and he sent a silent prayer that he would be able to return to his home.

The waiting was excruciating when finally, two days before the end of August, they received word that De la Cerda's fleet was leaving Sluys. So, the battle would take place in the Channel. The English fleet weighed anchor from Winchelsea on the Sussex coast among the sound of trumpets and cheering. The knights and nobles received wine as they prepared themselves for battle. It did nothing to soothe Ruadhán's spirit and he remained ill at ease. All his thoughts were of his homelands and Clémence. He prayed morning and night that she was receiving the advice and help she needed, and that all was well.

It was a full twelve hours before they sighted the Castilian ships, and getting late in the day, as they headed along the English coast, with a north-easterly wind blowing them closer.

"Christ's saints," Ruadhán murmured. "They're huge. Their masts are almost twice as tall as ours. Archers up in those boat-shaped structures at the top will have a grand day showering us with arrows."

"But they still only have crossbows," Stephen de Chesham replied. "And since they have the advantage of the wind, perhaps they will pass by without engaging."

"I can't see King Edward allowing that. By all accounts he's livid about the stealing of the wine and the sinking of our ships." Ruadhán was increasingly uneasy.

"Come, my friend, it is unlike you to be so wary. I see you've brought your shield along. That'll spare you from any arrows from above. You're one of the best swordsmen I know, so if we're boarded it'll be just the same as before and we'll see them off."

A roar arose around them and all eyes turned to the king's flagship, the *Cog Thomas*.

"He's going to joust with the lead Castilian carrack," someone shouted, and then "joust, joust" became a rousing chant.

"See! I told you, my friend. It's nothing but a land battle on the waves." Stephen laughed. "They may be larger and taller, but we have fifty ships."

Ruadhán watched with hesitancy as the enemy drew closer with full sails and speed from the wind at its rear.

The crash and splintering of wood was profound as *Cog Thomas*, with its deep hull, sharp bowsprit, and built up forecastle, rammed the leading enemy ship. Shouts of conflict rent the air before similar cries reverberated from other ships.

"Look! That topcastle has sheared from one of the masts," someone shouted as they watched men falling to their deaths into the churning sea.

"*Thomas* is listing," called another. "The force of the collision has sprung some of her seams."

We can't lose the king at this early stage, Ruadhán thought, but he knew better than to speak out loud and destroy the morale of those around him.

"They're boarding the Castilian," another said. "We'll win this day, yet, with Edward as our liege, his sons, too. They're fearless, and so shall we be."

A flash of light followed by smoke and an almighty *whump* made them all start. A cheer arose. "Is that the first-time cannon has been fired at sea?"

They watched as the Black Prince's ship followed suit, similarly bursting its seams with the crash of the collision. It looked as if they might be losing, but then they saw the Earl of Lancaster and his men boarding the enemy ship from the far side. Even from this distance the cry of "St George and Derby!" reached their ears and they saw the distinctive black armour of the prince as he and his men boarded the Castilian ship.

The *Michael* was on the southern side of the flotilla and along with the *Godibiate* was one of the last to engage, but a hail of arrows from crossbows rained down, along with lead weights. Ordinary seamen and some nobles fell. Others slipped as blood began to seep onto the wooden decking. The bowmen from the *Michael* aimed high and the air was filled with the thump of taught bowstrings released, followed by the hiss of the arrows' flight. Screams and hollow thuds followed, depending on where they landed. It wasn't long before grappling hooks exchanged and tied ships together, enabling men to clamber up rigging to land on the enemy ship. They cut halliards whenever possible to drop sails, bringing ships to a standstill, and then the fighting began in the close confinement of the deck.

Ruadhán had long since dropped his shield and instead used his sword, grabbing the blade with his left hand, he used the shortened form to stab, looking for any vulnerable spot he could find: face, throat, armpits, crotch, or the palms of hands, while his opponents did the same. In this mode he forced up a faceguard and thrust the blade with all his might, ignoring the scream and the blood that spurted over him. Kill or suffer the same was the rule.

As that man dropped, Ruadhán turned to the next. Several times he felt a nick but quickly became oblivious as he battled on. Using all techniques at his disposal, he even resorted to the *mordhau*, the murder stroke, grasping the blade of his sword with both hands and using the pommel to strike his opponent. Once the man was down, he deftly grasped it the right way to stab him and finish it.

Finding himself at Stephen's side, together they slashed and stabbed until their opponents fell. Stephen wrenched off one man's helmet before Ruadhán sliced open his neck, releasing an arc of blood. Suddenly feeling sick, Ruadhán could not echo Stephen's whoop of pleasured relief as once he might have done.

Numbers were thinning, and the cries of enemy soldiers flung overboard began to diminish. Ruadhán was weakening. Exhaustion and blood loss from several minor wounds was taking its toll. He was tired and thirsty. Thank the Lord that they were winning the battle with this carrack before another enemy ship came alongside. A captured ship was a good prize and if it was carrying silver and gold, as they thought, it would be a marvellous treasure.

That was his last thought before he turned to see a whiskered face at his side, swinging a spiked morning star club. Already covered in gore, the head of the weapon hit Ruadhán's breastplate with an almighty clang, taking his breath with it. Most of the weapon's spikes glanced off the good-quality metal of his armour, but the largest one at the club's head drove deep into his left arm between the plates of his arm harnesses. Already weakened, he fell.

Ruadhán was confused and disorientated. Was he dreaming or was this real? He was aware of his friend Stephen, but then he disappeared and a different face appeared. He heard odd snatches of conversation. Flashes of light; weird, distorted images that made no sense flew into his mind and out again before he could pin them down and interpret them; snatches of conversation.

"His breathing is laboured... I cleaned it ... wine before I sewed... You saw me bind ... herbs, but it's not healing..."

Ruadhán rolled his head and muttered. "Clémmie. Where are you? I can't... I feel..." A groan of agony rolled around the small room.

"He's got ... sweating, and I fear ... the flesh may have a necrosis."

Ruadhán made an effort and opened his eyes. A few moments of clarity followed.

"Undo the dressing. Let me see." It was Stephen. He noticed that Ruadhán was awake. "Ah! My friend, this is Signor Bianchi. I paid for him to travel with us since the choice was that or leaving him a prisoner in a flea-bitten hole in Deal, as we left the coast of Sussex. We'll soon be home in Lincolnshire. He's had a modicum of training in the first European medical school in Salerno before making his way north to experience more of the world. He ended up at Sluys, not expecting to be pressganged into joining the Castilian fleet. His captors let him come with me."

The surgeon did as Stephen bid and unwrapped the bandages.

"Christ's blood!" Stephen buried his nose in the crook of his elbow.

"It is corrupt, I fear," confirmed the surgeon.

"What's to be done?"

"I must take off the arm or the putrefaction will spread."

"He's a knight. He needs his arm for fighting. Surely there must be something else you can do?"

"I am sorry. The arm must come off if he is to stand any chance of life at all."

"But … but surely he will die if you take off his arm."

Signor Bianchi shrugged. "He will most surely die if I do not. What would you have me do?"

"Do it." Ruadhán's voice was strong. "Do it, man, before I change my…" He passed out again.

"Take it." Stephen turned away to pace the room.

"Hippocrates did this nearly seventeen hundred years ago. It's rare these days, but I have witnessed it."

"Are you saying that you haven't actually performed this procedure yourself?"

"The Catholic Church decreed there would be no taking of blood by surgeons, and they have only recently put it aside. Come, I shall require your assistance." He laid out the tools of his trade on a piece of clean linen.

Stephen looked at the various knives, a saw, tweezers, and needles with a reel of coarse thread. "Brandy, please," the surgeon said, without looking up.

When the drink arrived, Signor Bianchi took a slug. Stephen frowned. Then the surgeon raised his patient's head and gently poured some down his throat.

Ruadhán choked and muttered.

"Don't drown him first!" Stephen spoke loudly in his anxiety.

"I will treat him well. He is young, strong, and otherwise healthy. He stands a chance. I shall cut here." He indicated immediately above the bones of the elbow. "It's shattered inside, anyway, and will never function as a joint. I must take all the putrefaction and leave clean flesh to cover the end."

His knives were sharp. It took minutes to perform the operation, make his stitches and bind the wound after soaking it in more brandy."

Ruadhán lay pale and still, his breathing shallow. Only time would tell if he would survive the ordeal.

Clémence strode along the sun-baked path towards the church with a basket over her arm. She hoped that the few small offerings she brought would make a welcome change from the bread, fish and apples that was Agnes' main diet. She had put on a fresh dress and kirtle. She took joy in the day, but at the back of her mind was Ruadhán. Surely he should be home soon. News had reached them at the manor house of the battle's success, but she worried that she had heard nothing directly from him. Where was he?

Her thoughts turned to her father and brother. Mattie was gaining a reputation as a hard worker and more, as a skilful worker with wood. It was gratifying to see him among the other men and welcomed as an equal at last. Merek took comfort in his work, too, with long hours that meant he didn't have to spend so many in the small cottage he had shared with her mother, constantly reminded of the deep enduring love they had shared. He had voted to be among the last to have a new dwelling built so that he could continue working, but Clémence wondered if that was the best plan. He might do better in somewhere different where he could build new experiences and those memories might take on a semblance of happy reminders, rather than anniversaries which would never be repeated.Agnes received her basket with grateful thanks. Her voice had a rasping quality to it which Clémence put it down to lack of use. "Thank you, dear sister," she said. "God bless you."

"How do you fair?" Clémence asked.

"The monks are good to me. They care for me and some pray with me."

Clémence hesitated. "That other one, who disturbed you so deeply … are you now at greater peace?"

"Yes, sister. The other monks are all so gentle and kind. They seem not to know where that one went."

"And Daniel? Have you heard anything of him?"

"I have not, but I pray for his soul. I fear he performed a dreadful deed and I fear more that it was because of me. I pray fervently for his soul."

"Agnes, you were not to blame. Deodonatus lost his way, but it was not of your design."

Clémence left it there. She had said what had been on her mind for so long. "I fear for Sir Ruadhán. Please say prayers for him. I have not heard how he fares in so long and I am concerned." She did not own out loud the lacerating images that plagued her thoughts, especially at night.

CHAPTER 20

The pounding of hooves brought many of the workers to a standstill to gaze at the track and discern who rode with such haste. Someone called Clémence, and she hurried from the kitchens, hoping and praying that it was Ruadhán who returned at last. She was destined for disappointment for there was no shock of fiery hair on the head of the rider, whose hood had fallen back. Her heart began to pound. No good could come from a messenger who rode with such speed.

The man rode across the bridge, threw himself from his steed and hurried towards her. "My lady?"

Clémence curtseyed before this man who was clearly of noble birth. "I organise the manor, but I am not the lady here," she answered. "Our lord is away for King Edward and is not yet returned. May I offer you nourishment and something to quench your thirst? You have ridden hard, I see."

"I have a message for Mistress Clémence. Perhaps I may deliver that first?"

Clémence clutched at her throat. "I am she. I am Clémence Masson. Please tell me."

The man hesitated. "I am Sir Stephen de Chesham and I have been compatriot and good friend of Ruadhán Amundeville."

"You have been? Is he … is he…?" She could not bring herself to voice her fears.

"He lives, my lady, but if we had not captured the foreign ship and brought it to port, it may have been different. He is unwell, though, and follows in a litter."

Clémence breathed out. "Come. Let me offer some hospitality and tell me all. Leave nothing out, for I am strong and would hear every detail."

And she heard it all. She asked many questions before she was satisfied that Ruadhán had survived. Then, leaving Stephen in the care of her best people, she prepared for his arrival.

She had to wait a further twenty hours, but when the company arrived all was in readiness. Everything faded into the background as she concentrated on the man who lay in the wagon. He was sweaty and pale, his beard long and his hair tangled, but she caressed his face before ordering him carried to his rooms.

"This is Signor Bianchi, of whom I told you," Stephen said, and a man with dark hair stepped forward.

"Madame," he bowed his head. "I have done my best. It is now in God's hands."

"God's and mine," Clémence murmured under her breath. She turned back to the bed and cupped Ruadhán's cheek. "You shall not die, my love," she whispered. She watched his restlessness and was troubled.

"Undo these bindings, please." She looked at the surgeon.

"But my lady…"

"Now, please. I would look at the wound. It could do with a cleanse after the long journey, I'm sure."

She saw that the flesh was red and puffy. "Fetch the bread that I put aside. Ensure you bring the pieces with the most blue upon them."

"I cleaned it with liquor, my lady, and cauterized the blood pipes with a hot blade."

"I see you did a good job, Signor. Now we will continue to ensure the putrefaction does not spread."

When the mouldy bread arrived, Clémence supervised its application and ensured the doctor left the binding to a minimum. Throughout, Ruadhán remained in a deep sleep. After the company had left the room, at her instigation, she sat beside him. Later she asked for warm water and gently washed him while he slept, enfolding the clean linen around his prostrate form.

She repeated the process with the bread and bindings for several days, hardly leaving his side, bathing his hot face as he slept, changing the sheets as he writhed and groaned.

On the fourth day, Ruadhán opened his eyes.

"I've been dreaming of you," he said. "I dreamed you bathed me and whispered my name."

"I did," Clémence said. She gently swept his hair from his forehead and leaned down to kiss his cheek.

Ruadhán closed his eyes again.

Over the next days, Ruadhán was awake more and eventually able to sit by the fire and then walk a short distance. He was keen that Clémence accompanied him and they spoke constantly, but never about his missing arm.

"Perhaps, now things are so different and so many have passed away, including the Bishop of Lincoln … well, I wondered…" Clémence took a deep breath. "Perhaps we might find the money for Agnes to go and live in a convent or priory? There is a place not too far from here at Stixwould. It's a Cistercian nunnery. It's a small place and not wealthy. I think they would accept her and she would be content there."

Ruadhán nodded. "I will gladly pay the dowry if Agnes will consent. Do you think she might? I would hope she doesn't see it as breaking her holy vow."

"When last we spoke, she talked about having made her vow to the bishop as God's representative, and not directly to God."

"Then we will pursue that resolution."

Tears of relief came to Clémence's eyes. "Thank you." She knelt on the rushes before him and, grasping his remaining hand, she kissed it.

One evening, after she had completed her work for the day, Clémence saw Ruadhán walking in the gardens, and strode towards him. She carried her head high and was proud of who she had become. She fell into step alongside him. Most of the villagers had returned to the village and their new dwellings, and the manor was quiet.

"What will you do now that the plague had passed and all is so much calmer here?" Ruadhán asked.

"What will I do? Am I no longer needed here? You would cast me out?"

"No, of course not. But perhaps you are needed elsewhere? You always told me you wished to travel. 'Happiness depends on being free'," he quoted.

"Yes, and 'freedom depends on being courageous.' You see, I know my Thucydides. You gave me the opportunity here, while you were away."

Ruadhán smiled. "I forget how learned you are."

Clémence was silent for several moments, and then she looked at him. The setting sun set fire to the red in his hair and beard. His cheeks were once more rosy, the grey that had lain there for so long having been completely banished by her ministrations.

"I would stay and be here with you." She spoke quietly. "Before, I was impatient for life, I wanted to see what men see, but here, you have given me independence and allowed me space to flourish."

"I see," said Ruadhán.

"Do you still love me?" she asked. "If you say you do not, then I'll go."

He looked away. "I have little to offer. I am only half a man now." He looked down at his missing arm.

Clémence took a step towards him. Then, lowering her voice, she asked, "Do you love me?"

"Yes. Yes, I do love you, with all my heart." Tears appeared at the corners of his eyes. "Will you be my lady, dearest Clémence? Will you marry me?"

Clémence stared into his eyes. "We shall marry and care for each other. We shall live and love and laugh together."

She stepped forward into his embrace.

HISTORICAL NOTES

I have set this book on the estates of Grimsthorpe Castle in south Lincolnshire, where my husband is a tour guide. Today it is owned by Lady Jane Heathcote-Drummond-Willoughby, 28th Baroness Willoughby de Eresby, who was one of the ladies-in-waiting at the coronation of the late Queen Elizabeth II, and whose family have been Lords Great Chamberlains for centuries. The lineage is ancient, dating back to the crusades, and ancestors played a major part in English history, particularly with Henry VIII and since.

The land sits on the edge of the flat Fens of East Anglia, just where the land begins to rise into undulating hills. It became a prime target for Danish-led Viking raids during the eighth century. The Danelaw became a distinguishing feature of the area. Aspects of this pervaded into Mediaeval times and ensured that a much greater proportion of tenant farmers and craftsmen enjoyed greater freedom than serfs in other parts of the country. They were allowed to move about and to buy land, as Merek Masson did, for example. The legal system in these areas was also guided by Danelaw, even though the Vikings left nearly four hundred years earlier, as I have illustrated by the halimote fines in Chapter 10.

I formulated the idea of Agnes becoming an anchoress from the true account of a woman named Christine Carpenter in the village of Shere near Guildford in Surrey. The remains of her cell can still be seen in St James' church in Shere. Inthe church at Edenham, in Lincolnshire, is a small blocked-up window-sized niche from which my imagination ran.

Details of battles have been faithfully researched and written with as much accuracy as possible. The National Archives have limited information for this period but Jean Froissart, a medieval chronicler born in Valenciennes and who served Queen Philippa of Hainault as well as our King Edward III, wrote copious notes about the battle of Winchelsea. Froissart used his position to interview central figures and witness key events.

The Great Pestilence, or Black Plague, arrived in Britain via a ship docking in or near modern-day Weymouth in July or August 1348. However, for the sake of my timeline, I have it arriving a few months earlier than that. Records suggest the plague travelled at a rate of one-and-a-half miles per day and that once the fleas on the rats ran out of food they turned to feast upon humans, thus causing the rapid spread. King Edward III sent a letter around the country via ecclesiastical routes after his daughter Joan died on 2 September 1348, on her way to Castile. Although deaths for the general populous were not recorded, they were for the clergy, and it was estimated that in East Anglia, due to the heavily populated wool trade, the replacement of monks and priests rose to sixty-six per cent. Some of these may have defected their posts, but the majority were plague deaths.

Monetary records for *Vallis Dei* (Valley of God), which became known locally as Vaudey Abbey on the Grimsthorpe estate, are scarce, but it is suggested that, through the wool trade, the monastery became tremendously rich and in turn powerful. At one point the abbot was sent bearing messages to Llewellyn, Prince, of Wales, in the king's name. By the fourteenth century their income had declined for the reasons given in the story, but they maintained a position until the Dissolution, and by the middle of the fifteen hundreds it was finally in ruins. Charles Brandon, 1st Duke of Suffolk and good friend of Henry VIII, used the stone to build the castle which sits on the site today, but that story is for a future book. It's possible to walk to the site of the abbey within the Grimsthorpe estate. It's a beautiful and peaceful place. Sadly now, there are only grass covered mounds but there are two bases for pillars remaining and the Vaudey valley still has a stream which feeds the pond the monks would have used.

The family history of Henry de Beaumont is better documented. As I have indicated, his fighting prowess and original ideas for battle plans affected the successes in Scotland and at places like Crécy years later. His castle at Folkingham, north of Grimsthorpe, is no longer, but its position and ownership are without doubt. Interweaving fact and fiction takes precision. The manor house within the Soke of Folkingham, where Ruadhán and Clémence live, is completely fictitious.

A NOTE TO THE READER

Dear Reader,

Thank you so much for choosing this book. I hope you have enjoyed the story and the historical setting. I spent hours researching and learned a lot, although not much is written about some of the historical details. However, the process was fascinating, so I hope you consider I have captured the flavour of the period. Ensuring fact meets fiction seamlessly has been a challenge, but fun. I live five minutes from the |Grimsthorpe estate which is a beautiful place to walk. If you pass that way, I would encourage you to visit.

I must thank everyone at Sapere Books for their editing and for presenting the entire book so well. Their editing skills are truly exceptional. I'm very fortunate to have the backing of this team.

Please leave a short review or even a rating on **Amazon** or **Goodreads** if you have enjoyed reading *Mistress Of The Manor*. This, from knowledgeable people, is so important for authors' improvement and success, but also contributes to other readers' choice of book. I love to interact and answer questions from readers, so you are able to connect with me through Facebook, Bluesky, or X (Twitter) as RRCaraClayton

The next books in this mediaeval series will follow shortly, so do keep a watch out.

Kind regards,

Cara Clayton

Sapere Books is an exciting new publisher of brilliant fiction and popular history.

To find out more about our latest releases and our monthly bargain books visit our website:
saperebooks.com

Printed in Dunstable, United Kingdom

65438937R00122